ARCTIC WITNESS

HEATHER WOODHAVEN

LOVE INSPIRED SUSPENSE
INSPIRATIONAL ROMANCE

Special thanks and acknowledgment
are given to Heather Woodhaven for her contribution
to the Alaska K-9 Unit miniseries.

LOVE INSPIRED® SUSPENSE
INSPIRATIONAL ROMANCE

ISBN-13: 978-1-335-72263-8

Arctic Witness

Recycling programs for this product may not exist in your area.

Love Inspired
22 Adelaide St. West, 40th Floor
Toronto, Ontario M5H 4E3, Canada
www.Harlequin.com

Printed in U.S.A.

Fear thou not; for I am with thee:
be not dismayed; for I am thy God: I will strengthen thee;
yea, I will help thee; yea, I will uphold thee
with the right hand of my righteousness.
—*Isaiah* 41:10

To all the dogs who keep garden harvests
from going to the squirrels, thank you.

ONE

Someone was downstairs. Ivy West heard rushed footsteps before the security alert pinged on her phone. She set down the adoption papers she'd started to fill out. So much for a lunch break in her upstairs apartment.

The bottom of her boots slapped each wooden step as she hurried down to her post at the Nome Survival Mission, a small nonprofit store geared to help survivalists, preppers and anyone from the surrounding villages trying to withstand the harsh climate. Whoever was down there would hear her coming to help. She moved past the heavily stocked shelves of blankets and survival gear with a ready smile, only to find the room empty.

The wraparound windows provided ample views of the churning Bering Sea in front and the tundra of the Seward Peninsula on the sides. A few miles past the outskirts of Nome, the vast expanse brought a certain amount of comfort. She could never be caught off guard, and yet she'd been certain she'd heard someone walking around. No vehicles were out front.

A current of crisp September air hit the back of her neck. *Aha.* The back door wasn't fully closed. She opened the door fully to step onto the deck. Sometimes her visitors were skittish and traveled on foot. The mission frequently served as a first step for those who needed help getting to a women's shelter. Except, no one was outside but the musk oxen, grazing on the tundra brush. They needed to eat up. The wildflowers of the summer had already dwindled. Winter was at their front door.

She'd left Dylan's blanket in his car seat when she'd dropped him off with the babysitter. At thirteen months old, her foster child loved the messy teething biscuits. If she threw the blanket in the wash now, it'd be ready for when she picked him up this afternoon. She rushed down the deck stairs to where her Jeep and snow machine were parked on the back incline.

A warbling voice sent a shiver up her spine. Ivy reached for the pepper spray she kept fastened on the belt loop of her jeans, but relaxed when she saw it was a dog. With a gorgeous mix of gray and white, the thick coat of a Siberian husky fluttered in the wind as the animal stepped out from behind the vehicle. The dog's eyes softened while its white fluffy tail wagged hesitantly. Huskies rarely barked, preferring to howl or what sounded like an attempt at speaking.

She grinned. "Are you lost?" The gray at the top of its head formed a point on the forehead almost like a widow's peak, a unique marking that should help connect the dog with the owner quickly. The husky trotted toward the wild brush the musk oxen enjoyed. "Don't get too close. They're quick to use those horns, you know." She knew the canine couldn't understand her, but if huskies went to the trouble of attempting to speak, she wanted to return the favor.

The husky might be a missing sled dog, since the end of the famous Iditarod Race was held in downtown Nome. The start of the race was in Anchorage, where her ex-husband still lived. Roughly a thousand miles away. What would Sean think when she told him she was adopting a baby? He'd recently called, wanting her survivalist knowledge for a case. Ivy craved hearing his voice again, but since one of the reasons they'd divorced was his refusal to have children, she also dreaded telling him about Dylan. Her chest tightened like every other time she'd forfeited her dream of raising a family together.

The dog looked over her shoulder and waited a beat. Ivy placed a hand on her chest. "You want me to follow?" The husky took a few more steps toward the brush and again turned to wait. "Fine." She walked forward. The dog disappeared into the tall grasses and bushes. "I'm telling you right now, if you stir up a swarm of mosquitoes, I'm leaving." She followed the grass movement until the husky stopped and faced her.

On the ground, dark hair spilled out over the matted-down grasses. Ivy rushed forward. She dropped to her knees and reached for the woman's neck to search for her pulse. "Good dog!" This had to be the husky's owner. "Ma'am? Can you hear me?" Her fingers couldn't find a pulse. No breath. She ripped open the woman's coat to begin compressions.

Her gaze caught a dark red circle that spread from the center of the woman's chest.

Murder. Ivy's own heart pounded harder. This woman had been killed... But when? Her skin chilled. She stood, reaching for her phone. The husky released a short howl. She spun to see why, but lightning struck the base of her skull. Her bones lost all strength.

The grass, the house, everything turned white, then fuzzy as she tried to blink through the blinding pain. How'd the dog suddenly get over her head? Something grabbed her ankle and pulled. She struggled to raise her head, but blackness draped over her vision until her mind went silent.

Sean West stepped into the Alaska K-9 Unit headquarters with Grace, his Japanese Akita Inu partner, by his side. His bones felt heavy, having just returned from a recovery operation. They'd brought peace and closure to a missing man's family, and while he appreciated the purpose of handling a cadaver-seeking dog, success in such a mission brought a deep weariness. Being with the team, even in a boring meeting, would get his head back in the game.

Colonel Lorenza Gallo blocked his entrance to the meeting room. "You're back. I wasn't sure you would be in time. I need a quick word in private."

He tried to ignore feeling as if he were being sent to the principal's office. A quick glance over Lorenza's shoulders confirmed the rest of the team was waiting for the meeting to start. Grace tilted her fluffy fox-like head up at him as if wondering why they weren't allowed to join the rest of the K-9s. He shrugged and followed his boss a few steps down the hallway to her office.

"This will only take a minute," she said.

Sean wasn't sure if she was speaking to Denali, the retired K-9 husky who sat upright upon their entry, or him. Lorenza's silver pixie cut and tailored suit complemented the rest of her immaculate office, nothing out of place. She faced him and sat on the edge of her desk with her arms crossed. "Do you have your go bag ready?"

"Yes." Seemed like an odd question. He'd driven over two hundred miles early this morning, after the recovery case. He never knew where in Alaska he'd be assigned, as the elite K-9 Unit supplemented all law enforcement in the state. Sean's bag was always packed, though sometimes his extra uniforms awaited a wash, like now.

"We received a PD request for help. A missing woman, rural area, outside of police jurisdiction."

"You suspect a recovery is needed?"

The colonel stiffened. "I hope not. I've already assigned Helena and Gabriel to this case. I'll tell them to wait for you at the airstrip. They brought extra supplies for Grace just in case you're running low."

Sean tried to connect the dots. Lorenza wasn't supplying any of the details she usually loved.

"I didn't want to brief you over the phone," she said, as if seeing the silent question in his eyes. "And we're out of time. Helena will fill you in on the plane." She hesitated. "Sean, I'm sending you because if it were me… Well, that's what I would want."

His veins turned ice-cold, but his hunch could be off base. "Where?" he asked.

"Nome."

Sean's mouth went dry. She hadn't confirmed his suspicions, but he didn't want to take the time to discuss. He ran out of the building without another word. Grace trotted by his side. With the use of sirens, they made it to the airstrip within ten minutes. Helena Maddox and her Norwegian elkhound, Luna, stood outside of the cargo hold of the trooper-owned Cessna. Gabriel Runyon and his Saint Bernard, Bear, were already preparing to step into the aircraft.

Sean grabbed his two go bags, one specially equipped for Grace's needs, and jogged to the plane.

"You made it." Helena's shoulders dropped. "I wasn't sure you would. Are you okay?"

"The missing woman is Ivy?" He tensed the muscles in his jaw, determined to keep all emotion at bay at the thought of his ex-wife in danger.

Helena avoided making eye contact. "We don't know much except that a police rep went to drop off a donation and found the door open. Ivy was nowhere to be found. The PD thought it urgent enough to put in a call to Lorenza, partly as a courtesy to you."

Sean's heart went into overdrive. He nodded, glad for once that both Helena and Gabriel had gotten to know Ivy before the divorce. He wouldn't need to explain how out of character it would be for his ex to miss any meeting.

Gabriel gave Helena a side-glance. The man had an intimidating quality, no matter what expression, but that glance held a rebuke. Helena was supposed to tell him more, then.

"What?" Sean pressed. "What else?"

The other man's forehead creased. "PD spotted blood on the ground."

"We don't know if it's Ivy's," Helena added quickly. "It could be from an animal, for all we know."

Sean wouldn't allow himself to ruminate on a mission to find his own wife—ex-wife—dead. She *had* to be alive. He tapped the side of his leg, and Grace, without needing a command, jumped past the two troopers and their dogs into the plane. "Let's not waste any time."

Helena and Gabriel scrambled behind him into their seats. They each attached the special travel harnesses for the dogs into the seat belts. The pilot, another Alaska state trooper Sean didn't know, sat in the cockpit, checking instruments.

Roads across Alaska to Nome didn't exist. The only way there was by air, sea or dogsled. The ninety-minute plane ride was the fastest choice but torturous, as he feared his worst nightmare had become reality. As a search-and-rescue handler, Gabriel would take the lead on the case. Sean overheard his loud voice hollering over the noise of the propellers as he made calls throughout the journey to prepare for their arrival.

The wheels hit the tarmac and taxied up to three waiting trooper SUVs. The moment the pilot shut off the engine, Sean and Grace launched out of the plane. The vehicles weren't specially equipped for K-9s, but the dogs were trained for all manner of transportation, given the challenges the Alaska terrain could throw at them.

"Go east, and the Nome Survival Mission will be on our left. Can't miss it," Helena hollered over the wind. She and Luna jogged next to them and made for the middle vehicle.

The keys were left on the dash of each vehicle, just as Gabriel had requested. Sean flipped on the emergency lights and followed the other man's lead at full speed, barely registering the transition of cement to gravel and the beauty of the sea on his right. In a missing person's case in Alaska, every minute counted. And as Nome's history suggested, it was too easy for someone to disappear, never to be seen again.

They pulled in front of the mission. This was where Ivy lived? This small house in the middle of nowhere? Sure, they'd divorced at the point of barely speaking to each other, but lately they'd found reasons to talk more often. Almost as if they were becoming friends again. He'd imagined her as part of a community, not with musk oxen as her only neighbors. His stomach tightened to the point he needed to blow out a slow breath to keep the pain from registering on his face.

Gabriel stepped out of his vehicle, a hand up in front of Sean. "We got here in record time. Now, it's imperative we don't rush. There might be a scent Bear can grab as long as we're careful not to disturb the scene."

Bear's search-and-rescue specialty included being able to track scents, even in permafrost. That was likely why the colonel had assigned him to this case.

Helena climbed the steps to the deck that wrapped around the building. A lot of the houses close to shore were set on stilts to endure the floods and snow throughout the year. Thankfully, they weren't up against either at the moment, though flurries drifted onto his jacket from the gray clouds above. Helena placed her hand on her weapon as she stepped toward the ajar back door, swaying with the wind. "We'll check inside."

"If you see anything belonging to Ivy, bring it out, please," Sean called up to her. Maybe Bear could find her easier with a fresh scent.

"Understood." Helena hesitated. Luna stood at the ready, specializing in suspect apprehension, so if there was someone inside, the dog would find them. Helena pointed in the southeast direction. "Up here, I can see a matted-down path in the tall grasses. Might be from animals, but—"

"That's probably where our contact spotted blood," Gabriel said. "On it."

Grace did a little dance with her paws. Was she trying to tell him she smelled Ivy? Would she even remember Ivy from her days as a puppy?

"Found one spot of blood," Gabriel announced. "Small amount, but looks relatively fresh." He glanced at Sean. "Are you up for this?"

His mouth went dry. He knew what his teammate wanted from him. If he put Grace to work and she alerted on the blood, then they'd know that whoever had been on the ground was already dead before they were moved.

"Time to work." His voice came out in a ragged whisper. Grace's ears swiveled higher and her mouth fell open, as if smiling. He and Grace were often called to scenes where loved ones waited for news, so Sean had decided to use a relatively innocuous phrase to cue Grace. She dropped her nose to the ground and smelled the blood, then huffed, a sign she was annoyed.

Without alerting, Grace knew she wasn't going to get a reward. Sean fought against laughing. He'd never been so thankful. "If that's Ivy's blood, she was still alive before she left." Hope blossomed inside him with renewed vigor. "Can Bear track her?"

Before he could answer, Grace spun around and strained ahead, her nose frantically huffing and puffing in the matted path of grass. A second later, she sat down and looked over her shoulder at Sean.

Gabriel winced.

Sean pushed forward. A separate section of blood, dinner-plate in size, had caked in the grass underneath a pile of freshly pulled grass, as if someone had tried to hastily cover up its existence.

"Good work, girl," Sean said, but his voice shook. He produced her favorite chew toy, but as much as he tried, he couldn't offer a smile for his partner.

"It's two different people," Helena shouted from the deck. "I'm coming down. No one was inside the mission." Sean whirled around to see his colleague jogging toward them with a jacket in her hand that he recognized instantly. Gabriel took the jacket and offered it for Bear to start smelling.

"Why do you think it was two people?" Gabriel asked.

Helena pointed to the road. "From the deck, I could see a path through the grasses from here to the road." She pointed at the muddy areas. "It's more obvious with a view from above, but there were three people total.

Whoever did this dragged two people to a vehicle and drove through the grasses, likely on an ATV of some sort."

Grace dropped the toy and strained her nose east. Bear sniffed Ivy's jacket and immediately turned to the first spot of blood, not the second. Two different sets of blood meant there was still a chance his ex-wife was alive. "Best-case scenario, she's still with a murderer. We need to go now—southeast, it appears."

Helena studied the two men and nodded. "Someone needs to stay here and process the scene. You go ahead."

Sean fought against running through the grass to get to the car faster, as that might disturb the crime scene. He scooped up Grace's toy and moved to go. The dog stopped midgallop, sniffed something on the ground and sneezed. Sean leaned over. A pepper-spray can. He recognized the pink holder Ivy kept attached to her belt loop.

Helena grabbed her phone to start the lengthy process of photographing every angle and piece of evidence. "I see it. Go."

Sean ran the rest of the way to his vehicle and opened the door for Grace. He rolled down the window in the back seat to let his K-9 partner stick her nose out as they drove.

It was unlikely she would catch scents while he drove at high speeds, but not impossible. She could smell a drop of blood from a long distance.

Miles of coastline shifted into miles of tundra. As far as the eye could see, there was nothing but land and grazing animals. No sign of any humans or ATVs. Grace continued to strain her nose forward, sniffing wildly. In the rearview mirror, he could see Bear doing the same out the back of Gabriel's SUV.

A line of trees rose up out of the vast expanse of nothingness. Sean slowed down as the road disappeared. He bumped over the dirt, pressing onward. The tree branches brushed up against the sides of the vehicle. In front of him, a river rushed over rocks and boulders.

No bridge. A dead end.

He hit the steering wheel in frustration and Grace barked, her eyes squinting and her ears pointing in opposite directions, like she was asking him, *What's your problem?* His shoulders sagged as he waited for Gabriel to park behind him.

When Sean first took the job in cadaver detection, he focused on the noble act of bringing people much-needed closure, the type of peace his mom had never received when his uncle went missing on the Pacific Crest Trail. He kept the rest of the implications about his job at the back of his mind, never letting it grow louder than a dull hum. But now...

He couldn't find Ivy dead. He'd never recover. *Please...please let her be alive.*

Sean stepped out of the vehicle to face Gabriel. "Don't suppose you have a boat handy?" His teammate offered Bear a smell of Ivy's jacket. The Saint Bernard rushed forward, nose to the ground, through the tall grasses close to the first set of tree trunks.

Grace lunged forward and blocked Bear. She uttered a low growl, staring right at Sean. His mouth dropped. She never acted like that unless—

A click sounded. Two logs swung from opposite standing trees and smashed into each other, just above Grace's head. Sean crept forward, bending over until he saw the trip wire resting against the front of her legs.

"She was trying to warn us. Someone really doesn't want us to be out here," Gabriel said.

Sean blew out a breath, never more grateful for Grace. Because of the types of jobs they worked, she was trained to avoid a variety of dangers, usually wildlife and hunting-related. "Traps or not, we're Ivy's only chance."

Ivy's fingers moved and something soft brushed against her ankles. Weird physical sensations demanded she make the extra effort to open her eyes. A rotting wooden ceiling above her. A husky with a gray widow's peak stepped into view, looking down and sniffing her face. Ivy tried to twist away and sit up, but her hands refused to let her.

Her wrists were tied to a pole. Her heart jolted and her eyes widened, suddenly fully awake. She couldn't think clearly with the way her head throbbed. The husky shifted next to her. She managed to sit up and found herself staring into dark eyes surrounded by a black mask.

"So you're finally up." He was hunched over, his arms around a rolled-up rug. She didn't want to think about what was in the rug. The man dropped the rug and the tips of his fingers flopped over the edge. Ivy held back the scream building in her throat. He stepped forward and grabbed the collar of her sweater, pulling her close, her arms twisting against the pole. He studied her face.

She squirmed, trying to avoid looking into

his eyes, to get away from his touch. The friction of the rope against her wrists burned.

His eyes crinkled as if he were smiling behind the mask. "She gave you something, didn't she?"

"What? No. I didn't know her."

His eyes narrowed, maybe at her confusion. "I think you're lying. Just like she did. You can either talk on your own or be made to. Is that what you want? To end up like her? I'll give you a minute to think about it." He released her and straightened. The bottom of his boot connected with her chest, sending her backward.

Her head hit the floor, straining her right shoulder socket as her hands remained attached to the pole. She closed her eyes, fighting against the waves of pain firing in her temples, neck and arms.

"Come," the man said. The sound of a dog's paws against the floor followed with a door slamming, then silence.

It was now or never. She *had* to escape. Dylan had no one else in the world but her. She gripped the pole and hoisted herself up. A moment later, her eyes adjusted to the dim light streaming through the front slats of the poorly constructed shack door. The man had tied her up with bowline knots.

She grabbed the spot to break the knot with her teeth while tugging on the loop with her strained right hand. The ropes fell away. The stiffness in her back and legs fought against her intention to jump up and run. She hobbled to the front of the shack, shaking the feeling back into her legs, and peeked out the door. Without a weapon for self-defense, she needed to be fast if she ran.

Tree branches hung down low, almost blocking her view of the husky and the killer's back. *Trees!* There were no trees in Nome unless someone counted the Nome Forest, a name jokingly referring to the pile of used Christmas trees collected in January. The permafrost prevented trees from growing deep enough roots. The closest place with trees was either Pilgrim Hot Springs or the Niukluk River. Pilgrim Hot Springs took hours to get to, so she would guess she was closer to Council, an abandoned townsite across the river. Still, miles away from her place. Even if she sprinted her heart out, she couldn't last long. She bit her lip to keep hopeless tears from rushing from her eyes.

Her racing mind could only settle on one prayer. *Help!* She nudged the door open a little wider. Her abductor hunkered over a metallic boat. The husky looked back at her and her breath caught. The dog jogged to the front of the boat, vocalizing a solemn warbling moan at the man but pointing in the opposite direction, almost as if creating a distraction for her.

He stood. "What? What is it?" The husky continued to make noise. "Stupid dog!"

Ivy pushed open the creaking door, hoping the husky's song covered up the noise. She ran around the backside of the shack with a quick look over her shoulder. The killer spun around, no longer wearing a mask. Their eyes met. Towering at roughly six foot three with auburn hair and pale skin, he lunged for a gun resting on a nearby boulder.

She screamed and darted into the tree line. Something snagged at her foot and she tripped. When she jumped up, she spotted a rope on the tree ahead, and another rope from a nearby tree. She grabbed a rock and tossed it forward. A ball made of spiked branches swung down, right where she had been about to run. She twisted and sidestepped the trap, her heart pounding in her throat. She had to keep moving or die trying.

Footsteps crunched over leaves behind her. If she ran much farther, she'd be out in the open again, an easy target for shooting practice. She dropped low, crouching behind a crowded grouping of trees. Maybe she could hide and wait until the cover of darkness. Footsteps grew closer. She held her breath, not daring to move a muscle.

A hand closed around her nose and mouth. "Shhh."

She flinched and struggled to breathe. If she could just lift her foot and strike the instep of whoever had grabbed her... A fox-like beast stepped into view. It *couldn't* be. Grace? She relaxed. The hand dropped and arms spun her around to face—

"Sean." She wrapped her arms around his chest and pulled him tight. "But how? How'd you—"

He patted her back. "Get behind me, Ivy. We're not out of danger yet."

TWO

Sean pointed at Ivy. "Grace, protect." He stepped around her with a hand on his weapon and gave a nod to Gabriel, who was peering through the trees. "What do you see?" His first priority was getting Ivy to safety. The shadow of a man filtered through the thick section of tree branches.

"Alaska State Troopers. Hands up!" Gabriel shouted.

A dog or wolf in the distance howled. Footsteps could be heard, but he couldn't get a visual. The trees and brush were too thick to see far here. Were there wolves in there?

"It's a Siberian husky," Ivy whispered.

Neither Grace nor Bear were trained in suspect apprehension, but even if Helena had come with them, she wouldn't have been able to send Luna through the woods after the suspect with possible traps hidden in the ground and trees. A splash sounded, followed by a boat motor revving. A few moments later, silence draped over the woods. They remained at the ready, a few minutes more, until absolutely sure it was safe.

"Did you get a look at your kidnapper?" Sean asked softly. Now wasn't the time to reflect on the way she'd felt in his arms. He could feel her quivering hand at his back as she stayed close.

Her breath rushed past his neck. "Yes. Roughly six foot three, auburn hair, fair skin, maybe a little younger than us, but not by much. And he had a boat, but you probably figured that out by the sound of things."

"Was there only one man?"

"Yes. I mean, he was the only one I saw."

Gabriel blew out a breath and dropped his hand away from his weapon. "I think it's likely he just gave us the slip. Where does this river go?"

"It splits off into roughly sixteen creeks, but they get narrow pretty fast and some are dry by now."

"Your description will help a lot." Sean turned back around to face her. "We'll pass it to the troopers, the police—"

"The village safety officers," Gabriel interjected, swirling his finger around in the area like a lasso to indicate how far-reaching the description would go. There were so many native villages that a village officer was recruited at each one to keep in communication with state troopers.

"There are traps hidden around here," Ivy said. She pointed in the direction of the river. "I could show you where."

Sean had first met his ex-wife at a wilderness survival course. She'd been the instructor, and after the other participants had gone home, she'd run him through extra drills and answered all his questions. Traps were never part of the curriculum, but he believed in her ability to help find them. "Thankfully, Grace spotted something amiss on the way to find you and we missed one trap already. We'll catch this guy, Ivy."

"Sean, she's still bleeding." Gabriel took a step forward and peered around at the back of her head. "Ivy, we also found your blood back at your place. Did that man hit you?"

Fury radiated through his bones. He should've noticed she was hurt by now. It was his job to keep her safe, and he was failing her. Again.

She reached for the back of her head and groaned. "I think he hit me with a gun or something. I'm not sure. I blacked out, and when I woke up, my head was killing me."

She pulled her hand back around, covered in fresh blood. "Must have reopened the wound when he kicked me down."

The pink-and-green flannel shirt his mom had given her for a birthday a couple of years back had bits of weeds and dirt all over it. Now it had blood on the shirttail as she tried to clean off her hand. Her hair, in a low ponytail like she had on their first date, was also streaked with red.

He should ask more questions. Instead, his face grew hot. He searched the woods behind him for any sign of life, any clue. The monster who had hurt and kidnapped Ivy needed to be thrown in jail. Now.

"How long do you think you were out?" Gabriel asked.

"I… I don't know."

Not a good sign. Sean focused on the ground for a moment before he faced her. Ivy's health was the most important thing now, and he shouldn't need a fellow officer to remind him of that. Anytime a person lost consciousness from trauma for more than a few seconds, there was the possibility of complications, which meant the man could've killed her. Grace sidled up to her and pressed against Ivy's leg, as if trying to support her. Many dogs could tell if a person were about to have a seizure or a diabetic crash. Grace wasn't one to seek out attention or someone to pet her. What if the K-9 could tell Ivy was going to die soon?

"Hospital, now." He reached for Ivy's hand. Cold and clammy. "We can get you there faster than waiting for an ambulance."

"Agreed," Gabriel said. "We'll return tomorrow at first light. Might have some more troopers available by then to cover more ground." He twisted and headed in the direction they'd come. "We'll lead the way."

"Remember, I can help you look for traps." Ivy's voice was uncharacteristically faint. "If we step out of the line of trees, we'll need to focus only on the ground instead of both ground and branches. The farther away from the shack, the safer it gets, I'd imagine."

Sean moved her hand to his arm so she could lean on him for support. "He had you in a shack?" His words were clipped, and judging by the way her eyes widened, she could read his emotions. He stared ahead and made his expression blank. The last thing she needed to worry about was him. If they hadn't found her in time…

Gabriel waved them forward. "We'll come back and investigate the shack tomorrow, then. Let's get her that medical attention and get back to the SUVs before dark."

Ivy remained quiet as they walked. He had so many questions to ask, but he held his tongue. Gabriel would make sure to get the description of the suspect to the region's law enforcement. All the other questions could wait until Ivy was treated and feeling better.

They followed her advice and stuck to the tundra, far from the tree line and river. They weren't moving fast enough for his taste, but unless he was willing to ask Ivy to let him carry her, he would need to trust they'd get there in time.

The moment he spotted the cruiser, he rushed ahead to grab a blanket and some first-aid gear from the trunk. He ran back to Ivy. "Do you think you can add a little pressure to the back of your head while I drive, to slow the bleeding?"

"Probably a good idea." She seemed paler than she should in early fall, after a summer of enjoying nature. At least, the Ivy he knew would spend most of her waking moments outdoors. He helped her into the passenger seat and waited until she had the gauze and ice pack situated behind her head before turning his vehicle around. Gabriel set the pace in front of them. Within minutes, they'd hit the highest speed they could safely maneuver.

The only sounds in the vehicle were the occasional crunch of rocks underneath the tires. "I was surprised to see you," she said. "Happy but surprised." Ivy offered an encouraging smile in his direction.

"Same, but I'm not too fond of the circumstances." How many times had he almost taken a plane to Nome to see her but chickened out? He'd usually replay some of their most-repeated arguments in his head until it was no longer a temptation. Time and space were supposed to make her absence easier, but instead, his heart had never felt so raw and vulnerable. "Listen, uh, after we get you treated, I'd like you to take the first flight to Anchorage. You'll be safe there. You can stay at our place, our *old* place, I mean. At least until we catch this guy." He took a deep breath to slow the stammering.

"I can't, Sean." Her eyes were strained. Against pain, maybe?

"After you're feeling well enough to travel," he said. "I'll sleep on the couch." He'd overwhelmed her, then. "If you've seen the guy's face, you'll be much safer somewhere else. Doesn't have to be at our old place."

"Even if I wanted to, I can't. I have…" She worried her lip. "I have responsibilities here."

"The mission? I'm sure the nonprofit can find someone else to run the store." His peripheral caught her grimace. "I'm not saying you'd be easy to replace," he added with a quick side-glance. "I know that your survivalist expertise is sought—"

"Sean," she said again, this time her voice urgent. "It's not that. I have a child now."

He fought to keep his face neutral again, his focus on the road, even though his gut felt like it'd been used as a punching bag for half the day. She had a *child*? Since when?

He studied the road. Unless she'd changed personalities, Ivy West would not have moved on that fast with someone else. They'd signed the papers twenty-two months ago. People could change after divorce, though. He certainly had. A child, though?

Divorce had been the end of their marriage. But moving on and adding a child to the mix was like slamming the door on any potential hope for a rekindled relationship. Not that he had such hopes. He gripped the steering wheel and moved his foot from the gas to the brake as they crossed a bridge. So, she was taken. It'd take some getting used to, but the bottom line was he had a job to do. He could

remove the personal nature of their relationship out of the equation. The bomb she'd just
dropped changed nothing. He wasn't going to
leave town until he knew she was safe.

"A foster child," Ivy said. Sean's forehead
looked like it was doing push-ups with his
hairline. She'd seen his face try to mask emotion a million times, but his forehead always
revealed that he had opinions. He just wasn't
ready to share them.

Her heart went into high gear. The pulsat-
ing feeling of heat at the back of her head
distracted her. She faced forward in the car,
trying to keep the gauze in the right place, but
it stung too intensely to apply actual pressure.

Ivy tried to forget the way his jaw pulsed
the moment she said the word *child*. He'd
made his position on the matter abundantly
clear when they were married. The world was
too messed up to bring any children into it,
he'd argued. Maybe on her darkest days she
could agree to accept his argument, but she'd
never truly understood his unwavering stance
against fostering or adopting, especially since
he was a natural around children.

"So you can see why I can't leave Nome,"
she finally said after the long silence. "I've
been fostering for a while now, and I can't

abandon him. There aren't near enough qualified foster parents around here as it is. They
have to ship a lot of children to the lower
forty-eight—" She closed her mouth tight.
He didn't need to hear her rant on the subject,
no matter how passionately she felt. The details of her life weren't his business anymore.

The memory of the man in the shack in-
vaded her thoughts. No. She didn't want him
in her brain ever again. She could barely
think straight while her head throbbed.

Maybe Minnie Harkness, her babysitter,
would be willing to let her stay the night.
"You're probably right about tonight, though."
The creep had attacked her at her home. He
knew where she lived. "I think I'd feel more
comfortable if Dylan and I stayed somewhere
else, at least for tonight." She shifted slightly
in her seat. "Can we stop at the mission just
for a second? I really don't want to drive all
the way back here after getting checked out
of the hospital. I just need the car seat and a
few supplies."

Thankfully, she was used to living on little
and the stockroom below her apartment held
everything they'd need. As a last resort, she
could take Dylan to the bunker her parents
had gifted her, east of town.

Sean said nothing, but his knuckles were

turning white around the steering wheel. This was exactly why they could never work through any disagreement. Whenever he closed up like that, she knew it was better to move on rather than try to get him to open up. Which was exactly what she'd been trying to do in Nome before he'd shown up, wrapped his arms around her and—

Her shoulders sagged, remembering the relief of being rescued. And by him. *Why now, Lord?* "Wait. Were you already in town? On a mission? How did you end up finding me?"

"Someone came to give you a donation and noticed—" he cleared his throat with a cough "—your absence and the blood."

She didn't trust her judgment with the unrelenting pounding in her temples, but it almost seemed like his voice shook. They only sent Sean to the scene if they suspected… She felt her eyes widen as the matter-of-fact nature of his work hit her anew. "The troopers thought I was dead and sent you to find me?"

"No." He shook his head frantically. "Lorenza sent me as a personal favor. She wanted Helena and Gabriel to do the heavy lifting. I'm sure she thought I knew you well enough that maybe I could help locate you quickly. We didn't know about the murder victim at the time."

"Oh." The memories of the dark hair spread over the grass and the fingers that appeared out of the rolled-up rug caused an unbidden shiver up her spine.

"Did you see the victim?"

"Yes, but I don't know who she is." Her throat throbbed and she barely was able to whisper the answer. There were enough similarities in their appearance that it could've been her. "Shoulder-length hair, petite, approximately the same age as the man who attacked me." The desire to wrap her arms around her baby increased exponentially. The poor little guy probably wondered where she was. She never picked him up this late. Did Minnie have enough baby food for Dylan's dinner?

"It can wait for now," Sean said, his voice kinder, gentler. "We'll need to ask you for a full statement after you're treated."

The vehicle stopped moving. Ivy realized with a jolt that they were already back at the mission. This home she loved had darker windows than she remembered. Her shoulders hunched forward, hating the new vulnerability she felt. Mere hours had passed, but everything appeared different.

She was a strong woman, resilient and ready to be a single mother by choice. She couldn't afford to let a murderer ruin the new life she'd worked so hard to build. Her eyes stung as she continued to stare at the mission.

Sean rested a hand over hers. "Tell me what you need," he said softly. "I'll run in and get it."

The warmth and comfort enveloping her brought a different type of pain. She slipped her hand out from under his touch. "It'll be faster if I go. Sorry, I zoned out for a minute."

"You need to be seen."

"I will, but I'm sure the doctor is going to say I just need rest. Five more minutes won't kill me." Her breath caught at her careless use of the word. A woman had been *killed* here. Squaring her shoulders, she stepped out of the vehicle and flinched at movement in her peripheral.

It was only Helena, waving at her from inside the tall grasses. Her hair was longer than the short cut she'd last seen two years ago, but at least Luna looked the same. Sean's team acted more like family when they worked big cases together. She'd gotten to know many of the troopers at the picnics and barbecues. Ivy's confidence faltered. Did they hold a grudge against her? Even though they'd mutually agreed that their marriage wasn't working, friends tended to pick sides in a divorce. They'd obviously side with their teammate, Sean.

Helena's kind smile didn't seem to hold any animosity, though. Luna rushed out of the grasses and her handler followed behind her. "I think I'm done processing the scene. Sean radioed that you need something inside?"

"I just need to grab some supplies." Ivy tried to hustle up the stairs, not wanting to think any more about the events of the day. She grabbed the first container on the edge of the shelf. Emergency Survival Supplies, a kit she put together for any women on the run, might prove useful. She also picked a back-pack kit made specifically for toddlers, which would hold diapers, wipes and baby food.

Sean stepped inside the mission with Grace by his side. "I transferred our gear to your Jeep. I figured you might need to take your foster child somewhere after you're patched up at the hospital. Easier to drive your vehicle than try to put a car seat in the trooper SUV."

The man had a servant's heart. Even once they'd agreed to divorce, when they'd lived the remaining days of their marriage in separate rooms, he still made the coffee the way she liked it and took her Jeep to have the oil changed. Things were wonderful when they were in agreement, but when they weren't…

There was so much they could never see eye to eye on. Sometimes she wondered if she'd found Christ before their divorce, would things be different? Christian or not, people still divorced. She couldn't control his decisions. She turned away from Sean to give the stockroom one last look and refused to let her mind ruminate on what-ifs. "I think that's all I'll need for tonight, at least." Her gaze caught the front door. "The camera," she said, pointing. "I got an alert that someone had come inside. I don't usually check it because our internet is so slow out here, but if the attacker or the woman came through the front door, the camera should've saved the footage."

She reached for her pocket to pull up the camera app. *No phone, of course.* She glanced at the front counter where she usually kept her personal items, but her phone wasn't there, either. The murdered woman flashed in her head again. "I had my cell phone with me," she murmured, the memories becoming clearer. "To call 9-1-1. Did Helena find my phone in the grasses?"

"Not that I know of, but I'll ask."

Her stomach soured, and her muscles turned weak and shaky. She couldn't panic. "Sean, if you can't find my phone out there…"

Her voice shook and she fought to gain control. "That man has it."

She remembered the sensation of her fingers moving of their own accord before she woke. Her wrists still showed angry purple marks from the rope. What if he had used her thumb to access her phone? He'd have gained access to photos of Dylan. She needed to get to her baby. *Now.* She hefted the backpack up on her shoulder. But her muscles refused to cooperate, and her legs gave way. Hands pressed against her back, pushing her upright.

"Ivy?" Sean's voice sounded panicked.

She blinked intentionally, trying to focus, but everything was blurry. His arms cradled her neck and knees, and he lifted her to his chest.

"Dylan." The only word she could whisper before her brain flipped a switch and all went black again.

THREE

Sean paced the empty waiting room. Grace kept rhythm with him, tapping four staccato beats for each of his strides. She stayed with him for five laps across the twenty-foot room until she flopped down with a harrumph. If she had eyebrows, one would have definitely been raised. He leaned over and ruffled the top of her head. "You've had a hard day, too. Sorry I'm not taking this well."

A woman in blue scrubs walked out from Ivy's room, stopped at the nurses' station and turned to face him. "You're the husband?"

"Yes." Sean gave a flick of his hand, a simple thumbs-up that let Grace know the doctor wasn't a threat. The Akita sat at attention while he crossed the room to meet the doctor. "Ex-husband, actually."

The doctor gave a cursory glance at Grace. Before they'd entered the hospital, Sean had slipped on the dog's official Alaska State

Trooper K-9 Unit vest. Once on, Grace's uniform usually silenced any questions about a dog being in a hospital.

"Can you tell me Ivy's prognosis? She was in and out of consciousness on the way here… and likely hit on the head with a gun by her assailant at one point. Probably out for hours."

The doctor's forehead creased. "It's never good when someone has blacked out for that long. I can tell you she's extremely dehydrated. I'm waiting on the scans for any other diagnosis." She offered a kind smile. "Feel free to wait with her."

Grace padded along by his side as they walked down the hallway and into Ivy's room. Recessed lights glowed over the cabinets lining the wall. Ivy's head was wrapped in a bandage, and a tube extended from her arm. She waved her right fingers half-heartedly. Grace's tail flopped against the side of his leg. No doubt about it now—his partner remembered Ivy.

"You're awake. How are you feeling?"

"So much better."

He grabbed a chair and pulled it to her bedside. "You've got some color back."

She pressed her lips together and took a deep breath. "When I got knocked out, I hadn't had lunch yet."

Black coffee every morning, he remembered. She rarely ever ate anything before noon. Sean still enjoyed a big breakfast, but he'd appreciated the way she'd sit and sip from her favorite mug, two hands wrapped around the ceramic for warmth no matter the weather. Halfway through the mug, she'd pour in more coffee as a warm-up. She'd continue the routine for several more refills, but always set off to conquer the day with almost a full cup still left in the mug. It used to drive him nuts until he started turning her leftovers into iced coffee for the afternoons.

"What's so funny?" She tilted her head to the side. Grace did the same, mimicking her expression.

"Nothing." He'd forgotten moments like these. Strange, the small things he missed. He hadn't gone to the trouble of making iced coffee in almost two years.

"Can I use your phone? I'm really worried about Dylan." She glanced at the tube attached to her arm with a grimace.

"He's on his way here. I reached out to the foster care folks. Didn't take long before we found his social worker, and she had your babysitter on file. Helena should be escorting them both here as we speak."

Her shoulders relaxed and she sank into the

pillow behind her. "Thank you." She shook her head. "They might not let me take care of him if I'm in danger."

"They know you won't be staying home. Helena assured them we'd be taking charge of your security. For now, they're fine with it."

The way her eyes passed over his face, silently studying him, set the hairs on the back of his neck on edge. What was she thinking?

"Thank you," she finally said. "I'm ready to give my statement. I'd rather get it done before Dylan gets here. He's thirteen months but picks up on everything. He'll be able to tell I'm upset." She took a deep breath.

Sean pressed the voice-record feature on his phone. "Are you sure you're ready?"

"It's like a nightmare. Some parts are more memorable than others. That husky I told you about helped me escape. They're really loyal animals, and looking back, I think she was trying to get help for her owner…"

Sean watched Ivy's forehead tighten and lips purse, fighting off emotion. He leaned forward and gave her hand a squeeze. It was too natural to reach for her. He released her fingers just as fast. "Are you sure you're up for this? We can wait for Helena and—"

"Yes, I'd like to get it over with while my memory is fresh. The Siberian husky made me wonder if the murder had something to do with the Iditarod. We have a few teams that train around here. Although, the killer didn't seem to have the type of fit physique most mushers have, so maybe the woman he killed was the musher. Or the husky was just a pet." Her eyes focused on the wall across from her as if the day's events were being projected there. "I think the woman came to the mission because she wanted survival gear from me. Maybe to run away from the killer. But he found her before that could happen."

"We'll investigate all those possibilities. We found your pepper spray. Did he attack you first before he knocked you out?"

"No. It was like he came out of nowhere. I was about to call 9-1-1."

"Maybe he was preparing to transport the body, or he hid in the grasses when he heard you approach."

"When I woke up, he said something strange. He wanted to know if she gave me something." She squeezed her eyes tight. "I can't remember his exact wording." She opened her eyes and shrugged. "I had no idea what he was talking about. For all I know, he was out of his mind."

"Bye-bye…bye-bye! *Bye-bye!*" A little

boy's voice was getting louder and louder and rang through the hallway.

Ivy sat straight up, a smile radiating across her beautiful face. "Dylan? I think that's him." She laughed, her eyes bright. "When he starts shouting *bye-bye*, it means he doesn't want to be here."

An older woman with curly, shoulder-length black hair highlighted with silver streaks stepped inside the room. She was hunched over, holding a little boy's hand. "Would've been here sooner if he'd let me pick him up and carry him. He's in one of his independent moods today, Ivy. Just like his mama. You doing okay, sweetie?" Helena and Luna stood behind the sitter and child.

"Thanks, Minnie," Ivy said. "I think I'm going to be okay. Just a big knock on the head is all."

Understatement of the year. His own legs felt weak remembering the moment she pulled her hand away from her head, covered in blood. The boy ran forward in a waddle, tripping over his shoes, hands outstretched, determined to reach Ivy. Sean could see the same determination to reach him in Ivy's eyes. She sat up and tried to lean over the side of the bed. But she shouldn't be picking him

up before the doctor gave the all clear. The
boy froze midrun, blue eyes wide. "Doggy!"

Grace flopped her tail from side to side but
remained in place, as Sean's splayed fingers
directed. Most of the Akita Inu breed were
only trained and used as guard dogs for law
enforcement and not recommended as family dogs, but the troopers had rescued Grace
from a shelter as a mixed-breed puppy. While
mostly Akita Inu, especially in appearance,
her DNA revealed a hearty mix of golden
retriever, which probably accounted for her
amazing smelling abilities and fondness for
little people.

Sean scooped the boy up. The moment the
bundle of energy was in his arms, the striking shade of Dylan's blue eyes and dark blond
hair were hard to ignore. It was like looking
at a photo of himself at that age. Sean froze.
The toddler stared into his face, as well. Did
the boy see the resemblance, too, or was he
stunned into silence by the fact a strange man
had picked him up?

Math wasn't Sean's strong suit, but they'd
been divorced twenty-two months. If Dylan
was thirteen months old, was there any possibility that—

"He's only been with me six months," Ivy
said softly, reaching her hands out and of-

fering a sweet smile Dylan's way. "But he's already got me wrapped around his little finger."

His ex-wife knew exactly where his mind had gone in that brief moment, Sean was certain. She'd read his thoughts and attempted to spare him from an embarrassing conversation in front of his coworkers. Whether he should thank her later or not, he hadn't decided. He preferred to avoid potential triggers that would reopen past disagreements.

The boy strained in his arms, eager to go to Ivy. Sean, careful to avoid the IV, rested Dylan in her lap. The little hands reached for Ivy's neck. He wrapped himself around her, while resting his chubby face against her chest. Sean's heart practically exploded out of his chest in a way he couldn't understand.

He'd decided three years ago that children would be out of the question. In his line of work, he didn't need any new vulnerabilities. At the time that he realized he'd need such strict boundaries, Ivy was already in his life, but his job required everything else of him. He'd turn down any new opportunities to make him susceptible to weakness.

It wasn't that he didn't like kids. He enjoyed them a lot. *Other* people's kids. He could make them laugh, then walk away without getting too attached…

Dylan and Ivy pulled back from their hug, beaming at each other. Despite himself, his heart melted again.

Sean turned to Grace to get his bearings. The dog, the team, the job. That was his life. And right now, he needed to focus on finding the murderer so he could leave Nome with the knowledge that Ivy was safe. The faster he did, the better.

Ivy followed Minnie down the hallway of the Golden Dreams Bed and Breakfast until she stopped at a door to the left. "Here's your room," the older woman said. She used an old-fashioned key to unlock the door. "I'll make sure someone brings down a portable crib for Dylan."

The room managed to feel bright and airy while capitalizing on Nome's other claim to fame, the rush. While most famous for the gold rush of the late 1800s, the past few years had brought a second rush of sorts. At least, enough to draw the attention of fortune hunters and reality shows. The lamps were crystal containers of what appeared to be gold glitter, the gold bedspread was complemented by the blue curtains that looked like rivers, and even the sink basin resembled a gold panning bowl. If it weren't almost midnight, combined with a bandaged head and painkillers in her system, she'd have been thrilled by the decor. "Thank you, Minnie. This is lovely, but are you sure I'm not taking business away from your daughter?"

"The troopers are paying for the lodging," Sean said, appearing behind Minnie with a backpack slung over each shoulder. "You are a witness to a homicide and a victim of kidnapping. We need to make sure you're safe. We take our job seriously." He stepped past Minnie and opened the adjoining door.

Helena appeared on the other side of the door. There were two beds in the female trooper's room and her K-9 had already commandeered one of them. "We'll be here. If you need anything, Luna and I can make another run into town." She pointed at Sean. "I just received some good news from the pilot we commissioned. He's already delivered the evidence to the lab, and I've given Tala a heads-up that we need this bumped up to priority status."

"Oh, I remember Tala," Ivy said without thinking. She might have been proud she remembered so many of their team members, but she doubted they cared if she knew who their go-to forensics scientist was. Tala Ekho worked for the Alaska State Crime Lab, only a couple of miles from the K-9 team headquarters, and she assisted with most of the K-9 cases. Ivy had been introduced to the woman at one of the picnics and was immediately drawn to her, perhaps because Tala seemed as if she was an outsider, too.

Sean's eyebrows rose. "You only met her once. I'm impressed."

"Hopefully, we'll have some new leads soon. And we're working on tracking your phone, Ivy." Helena offered a friendly smile. "So far no pings, but we'll keep at it. As soon as the phone is somewhere with a signal, we should get a lead."

"That is good news. I don't like the thought of him having my phone." She couldn't shake the weird memory of the man grabbing her hand before she was fully awake.

"I finally made it." Gabriel stepped past Helena, as if joining a late-night party in Ivy's room. The thought almost made her laugh aloud. The trooper carried a jug of milk and a bag of baby food and snacks, while also loosely holding a leash for Bear to stay at his side. He set down the items on the dresser. "Did you know they sell ATVs in the produce aisle? They're sitting right there in between the cucumbers and the shelves of bread. And *eight dollars* for a gallon of milk?"

Ivy snickered, imagining his reaction. "Thank you, Gabriel. Welcome to Nome." Such a beautiful and remote area came with a price. All groceries and supplies had high transport costs added. And their grocery store didn't only carry groceries. She'd gotten used to vehicles in the veggie aisle without much thought.

"Doggies, doggies, doggies." Dylan squirmed in her arms, reaching both hands out, opening and closing his fingers, as if he wanted to squeeze the K-9s like stuffed animals.

"Sorry, buddy. Bear's head is almost the same size as your entire body. I'm not sure he'd appreciate you pulling his hair out." Ivy perched on the edge of the bed so he could see the dogs better.

Sean threw a thumb over his shoulder. "Gabriel and I will be stationed in the rooms across the hall."

Minnie stepped back into the room. "I may not technically own the place, but being the mother of the owner does have its perks." Minnie's son-in-law, Ben Duncan, appeared with the folded-up portable crib. "It's been a slow tourism year, so they're happy to have you." Ivy knew Ben, but not very well. "Okay, we'll let you get your rest," Minnie said.

Ivy's cheeks heated as she faced the woman who was not only Dylan's babysitter but her closest friend in town. Minnie had actually been the one to lead her to Christ. The freedom and love that Ivy found in the Gospel was one of the reasons she wanted to spend her life helping others.

Everyone left the room except Sean and Grace. Helena's door remained slightly ajar as Sean set up the folding crib. Ivy sat down on the edge of the mattress. Her bones felt like they weighed twice as much as usual. Grace rested her chin on Ivy's free knee. "Oh, you really do remember me." Ivy helped Dylan hover his little hand on top of the Akita's head. "Gentle," she said.

While Sean had always warned Ivy that Grace was a partner and not a pet, the dog still had managed to steal her heart. It had been so hard to say goodbye to Grace.

"Is doggy?" Dylan asked, twisting his face until they were nose to nose. Dylan had developed the habit of getting in her face, making sure she had no choice but to answer him.

"Yes. Doggy's name is Grace."

"Yace!" Dylan attempted the name with a nod. Grace wagged her tail and let her tongue

hang in response, sending him into a fit of giggles. He rubbed his eyes, so exhausted. Ivy snuggled her little boy and swayed side to side, too tired to stand.

"I think we're set here." Sean checked each rail of the crib to make sure it had locked correctly. The small attention to detail was like a punch in the gut she wasn't prepared for. This was what he would've been like as a father.

"Are you okay?"

"Fine," she answered, pushing past the tightness in her throat.

His eyes narrowed. "I'm familiar with traumatic brain injuries—"

"Mild," Ivy interjected. "The doctor said it was a mild injury. He said if I rest, I'll be fine."

"He said most likely. It's not a guarantee. You have to tell me or Helena if you have headaches or nausea. Promise me?" His eyebrows lifted and then lowered as if he realized he'd crossed a line. Her husband could ask her to promise, but it was plain odd for a trooper to ask in that way. "I mean, I hope you take your health seriously. Please ask for help if you need it."

She sighed. "I understand and I will. I'm about to fall asleep sitting up."

Thanks to Minnie, Dylan had already been fed and changed into pajamas.

"Then let me help you." Sean's expression softened, staring at the toddler. She glanced down to find him asleep on her chest. Sean bent over and lifted him from her arms. The coconut scent of his hair caused her to inhale automatically. She loved that smell.

Sean turned and lowered him down in the crib carefully. Dylan blinked his heavy eyelids and began babbling, half-awake, his normal routine to drift off to sleep. At least he hadn't started singing. He really enjoyed babbling songs, though she was probably the only one who could recognize them.

Grace turned and sniffed the mesh panels of the crib. "Not now, Grace," Sean whispered. Dylan giggled but thankfully didn't stand back up.

"I'm thankful, Sean. I really am. Now that I'm safe, I feel certain that when I interrupted that horrible man's plan, he acted in the heat of the moment when he abducted me. He's headed as far from here as he can if he's smart. I'm sure I'll never see him again." Even saying so aloud helped ease the hum of anxiety in her stomach.

Sean picked up the backpacks he'd left by

the door. "I don't like to remind you, but you did see the man's face."

"And Alaska is *huge*. I want him behind bars just as much as you do, but the point is, he has a chance of never being caught. And if that's the case, I'm safe. I'll take you guys to the shack tomorrow and hopefully you'll find enough to track him down, but I don't think it'll be anywhere near here."

Sean tapped his leg and Grace returned to his side, a stark reminder that the dog's loyalty to Sean and the job always came first. "Get some rest, Ivy. We can discuss the next steps in the morning."

There was wisdom in waiting until morning to make any decisions, but old hurts and longings rose to the surface at his abrupt end to the conversation. Like pausing an old movie before she'd seen the ending. "Good night, Sean. Good night, Grace."

He slipped out the door, and within minutes, Ivy had put away the milk and groceries into the mini fridge and readied herself for bed. Focusing on tasks that needed to be done helped keep the churning thoughts at bay, though she feared it would be harder now that her head was no longer distracting her with throbbing pain.

Helena's hotel door was left an inch ajar,

but her light was already out, as well. Ivy clicked off the lamp and snuggled under the covers. Minutes of sleeplessness turned into an hour of staring at the patterns in the ceiling. She was growing more awake, not less, despite the exhaustion. Maybe it was the painkillers' fault.

The whine of a door hinge sent a shiver up her spine. The moonlight seeped in between the sliver of the two curtains. A shadow moved across the wall closest to Dylan.

A man was making his way to her bed.

FOUR

Sean tightened his fists for a count of five and released. He'd already changed into his K-9 Unit sweatpants, but it was hard to relax when he kept replaying every interaction with Ivy. Fatigue finally won out. He focused on his breathing as sleep took his mind.

Grace growled, a low rumble in her throat that sent him jumping out of bed, all promise of slumber gone. She never made that kind of noise without a reason. "What is it?"

Grace trotted to the hotel door. She barked another deep and impressive growl. Sean grabbed the gun on the nightstand. His heart pounded in his head as he yanked the hotel room door open. The hallway was pitch-dark. Why? The hallway light was on when he'd gone into his room.

Another bark sounded, this one higher pitched, and not from Grace. A woman screamed.

Helena yelled, "Attack!"

A baby wailed. *Dylan?*

Sean lunged across the hall. A sliver of light led him to Ivy's door, left ajar. "Alaska State Trooper," he yelled as he burst into the room. The baby's cries accompanied Luna's frenzied barking. Light from the street streamed in from the open window. Luna was halfway through the window, her head poking out.

Helena tugged on her K-9's collar. "Off, Luna." The curtains fluttered into the room, along with the cold arctic breeze. The dog sat and Helena closed the window and flipped the lock.

While still dim, the light from the street highlighted Ivy's form, hunched over and pulling the screaming Dylan from out of the portable crib. She straightened and whispered, "Shh," in a soothing pattern.

Lights flooded the hallway. Sean spun around to find Gabriel and Bear in the doorway.

"What happened?" Gabe beat him to the question.

"A masked man entered through the hallway," Ivy said softly. "Shh, it's okay." She went back to comforting her baby boy.

"Ivy screamed. I ordered Luna to attack, but the assailant made it out the window."

Helena spoke rapidly. "I think Luna bit his wrist but didn't get enough of a grab to hold him. By the time I got to the window, he was gone."

"Do you think we can find a scent? Should I go?" Gabe asked.

"Let's try. I'll go with you. If we catch sight of him, I'm sure Luna will want a second chance to take him down." Also dressed in her official sweatpants, Helena ran into her attached room with Luna by her side, presumably to slip on her shoes on the way out. Gabriel met her in the hallway, and they ran together, out the door.

The adrenaline pulsed hard and fast in Sean's veins, begging him to search with his team, but Ivy needed him. And Bear and Luna were more suited to the task.

"I know you probably want him to go to sleep, but I need to ask you some questions first." Sean found the light switch and lit up the room. Ivy dipped her head, her cheek pressed against Dylan's. "It's okay," she whispered. The baby's cries had faded into staccato sniffing and shuddering gasps.

She rubbed Dylan's back. "Oh, honey, I know. It was scary. You're safe now." She kissed the top of his head.

A memory of his first recovery with Grace,

after an earthquake, made an unwelcome appearance in his mind. He blinked it away. "I need to know exactly what happened tonight."

Even as he asked for more details, he knew the most important fact. The killer definitely hadn't left the area, and Ivy was still in danger. All the other questions made background noise in his mind. The killer had figured out her room and how to get inside without being detected.

He'd driven Ivy's Jeep here, but her vehicle blended in with the many other Jeeps in the lot. Helena and Gabriel had also parked their trooper vehicles in the parking lot. Law enforcement vehicles were a deterrent for any "normal" criminal. In his experience, the more desperate a criminal, the more dangerous.

His boss would want him to make finding the murdered victim a priority tomorrow. But now that Ivy had been rescued, once he and Grace found the victim, the colonel would likely take him off the case and leave other troopers to track down the killer. The truth hit him in the gut. Even if he had to take time off, he wasn't leaving Nome until he knew Ivy and Dylan were safe.

She swayed from side to side, still attempting to lull Dylan back to sleep. "I need to keep my voice light, like I'm happy, or he'll get worked back up again."

"Give Dylan to someone else."

Her lips pursed. "Excuse me?"

"If you want to be a foster mom after we find the killer, you still can. But right now, you're not safe. The baby isn't safe. Let someone else foster him and go to Anchorage."

"Give him *back*?" Ivy's eyes went wild and she clenched her jaw. But when Dylan turned his face up to her, she forced a strained smile.

Sean's chest tightened. The words had come out without a filter, again. "I could've been a little more tactful, but the bottom line is still true."

"While I agree that Dylan's safety is paramount," Ivy replied stiffly, "I can't just *give him back*, as you say." She turned away from him and set the boy in the portable crib with a new bottle. Dylan, though, had no interest and climbed up to standing, reaching for Grace, whose tail was just out of reach.

Ivy took a step closer to Sean. "I will contact the social worker first thing in the morning to keep her updated and decide what is best for Dylan, but I'm not going back to Anchorage. I'll go to the bunker."

"In the middle of nowhere?"

"All the more difficult for that—" she gestured to the window "—man. No one knows about the bunker. Which makes it almost impossible for any danger to find us." She blinked away the new sheen of tears forming in her eyes and stared at the golden carpet below her bare feet. "Sean," she said, almost in a whisper, "I appreciate you coming all this way and finding me. I really do. I know you're trying to keep me safe, but I'm a mother now, whether you like it or not. And I'm not your wife."

His internal temperature rose ten degrees on the spot. He'd let his desire to keep her safe rule his thoughts and feelings, instead of acting like the professional he was. At least Helena and Gabriel weren't there to witness his rash behavior, ordering her around like that. "You're right. I'm sorry."

Ivy's forehead wrinkled and her mouth dropped open. Grace looked up, her mouth also slightly agape at him. "Come on. It's not as if I've never apologized before." He chuckled, hoping his cheeks weren't turning red.

"True. Just a new speed record." She offered a small smile.

"I suppose I deserve that." One of his greatest regrets was how he'd handled disagreements in their marriage. He wanted to think he'd changed for the better, grown up since she'd left. And yet, the instant fear gripped his heart, he'd tried to lay down the law without so much as a conversation. Would he really have given a stranger the same advice? Maybe, but he would've asked a lot more questions. And he would've respected their input first and suggested a new course of action in a more delicate manner.

But even after the adrenaline of the incident and the argument began to fade, he still thought his plan was best. "As your…" He didn't want to call himself *the ex*. But did he have the right to say they were friends? "… former husband," he finally said, "I am asking you to reconsider coming to Anchorage. I think tonight is proof this man has no plans of leaving a witness alive."

Her face paled. Dylan giggled, averting their attention. Grace swished her bushy white tail left and right, barely out of reach of the boy's greedy little fingers. He cackled, laughing so hard he fell down to sitting in the crib and reached for his bottle. It proved impossible not to smile in response, which made it harder to return to the subject at hand.

"As a state trooper responsible for your safety, I'd like to place Grace in your room for the rest of the night as added protection."

"And—" Helena's voice rang behind them

"—you're switching rooms with me. Our search fizzled about two blocks away. He must have had a vehicle waiting."

Gabe and Bear appeared behind her and Luna. "The housekeeping keys were stolen from behind the front desk."

"Your babysitter, Minnie, signed us in," Helena added. "They do things old-school here. Paper and pen at the front desk. So when—"

"He managed to get her keys and her room number?" Sean crossed his arms across his chest.

"Oh, please don't tell Minnie it was her fault," Ivy said. "She would never forgive herself for putting us in danger. I know it wasn't on purpose."

Sean sighed. He agreed with a nod.

Gabe checked the window lock a second time. "Let's get the room switch done and see if we can catch a little shut-eye before sunrise. We'll look for new accommodations tomorrow."

Sean had several objections. He held up a finger. "But—"

"We've informed the local PD," Helena said. "They're putting a uniform in front, and they've got another officer canvassing the town." She flashed an encouraging smile.

"If he does manage to come back again, he'll find Luna here instead of Ivy. We'll get him before you know it."

He couldn't share her enthusiasm. The killer had evaded three trained officers and their highly trained K-9s. Until he was caught, sleep wouldn't come easy.

Ivy woke to the sounds of a truck's backup beep outside her room. She sat up and glanced at the clock. Already nine in the morning? By the time she'd switched rooms with Helena, it had been after 1:00 a.m., but she never slept this late. Even though it had brought her comfort when Sean ordered Grace to protect her, hours had gone by before she'd finally drifted to sleep. A quick peek confirmed the dog still rested, spread eagle, from her spot in front of the door. She'd often wondered, even when Grace was a puppy, if she dreamed that she could fly while sleeping in that position.

Her stomach growled. Grace's eyes flashed open. "Sorry, girl." Just this once, Ivy planned to indulge in the biggest breakfast the B and B offered and didn't want to sleep away her chance. Careful to move quietly so Dylan would remain asleep, she tiptoed toward the bathroom to get ready. Grace popped up, took a few steps and turned sideways, her posture regal, effectively blocking Ivy's path.

Ivy tilted her head back and let out a breath of exasperation. Of course, Sean's dog would take the protection detail a little *too* seriously. Just like Sean would. "I promise I'm not trying to escape," she whispered. She pointed to the bathroom. Grace took a step backward and plopped down again, apparently satisfied.

After getting ready in record time, Dylan began to stir. Ivy heard a tap at the adjoining door, slightly ajar for Helena's easy access. "Come in," she called. Before the door could open, Grace sprinted across the room and sat at attention at the door, sticking her nose into the space.

"Just me, Grace. At ease." Helena poked her head inside. Luna's head thrust past the door right below her knee, and the two dogs huffed at each other, as if in greeting.

Dylan laughed at the exchange. "Yace and Doggy."

"That's right." Helena offered him a grin. "Sean is waiting in the hall to take Grace for her morning walk and meal. If you two are ready, I'm to accompany you to breakfast. We have today's logistics to discuss."

Ivy nodded. "No problem."

"Come on, Grace." Helena disappeared

from view for a moment. Meanwhile, Ivy grabbed the diaper bag Minnie had returned to her last night. The zipper wouldn't close on the bag, overstocked with the baby food and snacks Gabriel had been kind enough to pick up last night. She had yet to open the emergency bag of supplies she'd brought from the mission. A relief, too, as she might need them once they got to the bunker. Dylan's rosy cheeks and beaming smile squeezed her heart tight. How long would they have to hide?

"Okay, Sean and Grace will meet us at breakfast in a few minutes. Ready?" Helena asked.

She looked past the trooper, fully dressed in the blue uniform, and remembered the shadow that had moved across the wall. Ivy had forced herself to wait until the intruder had creeped past the crib to make sure he wouldn't try to grab Dylan if she reacted. She'd bided her time as the man stepped closer, her heart in her throat, while praying fervently for help. Only when he'd reached the foot of her bed had she allowed herself to scream.

"Are you okay?" Helena reached out and touched her shoulder. "You turned white as a sheet."

"Yes. Sorry. I'm fine." Even though God had answered her prayer and help came in time, she still couldn't shake the helpless feeling. She'd always thought she was strong, but right now she wanted to do exactly as Sean suggested. *Run away.* Except she couldn't do that without Dylan, which took time and paperwork. Besides, she wasn't sure her heart could handle returning to the place she'd lived with Sean. So much hope and heartache experienced in one place. At least she could take Dylan to the bunker. She'd had the place approved during the foster application process since her parents stayed there when they visited. The bunker would be safe.

She kissed the smiling boy on the forehead, placed him on one hip and lifted the strap of the bag on her shoulder. "Rough night of sleep is all. Can't complain. You all got the same amount, too."

Helena laughed and stepped aside for Ivy and Dylan to walk with her to the door. "You'd think I'd be used to sleepless nights, but I'm not. I just appreciate the peaceful ones." Luna took a giant yawn, triggering another squeal of delight from Dylan.

"Great timing, Luna." Helena waved them forward and locked the door behind them.

They walked down the hallway, a tight fit all together.

"With everything going on, I never got a chance to say it's good to see you again, Helena. How are you?" Ivy realized she was holding her breath, wondering if the other woman would give her a cold shoulder if she tried to get friendly.

Helena surprised her with a genuine smile. "I'm good. I recently got engaged."

Her jaw went slack. If Helena's raised eyebrows were any indication, Ivy's surprise seemed unwarranted. She'd been under the assumption that the only people on the team who were married must have met prior to their K-9 specialties. A few months into Sean's K-9 duty, he'd changed. Came home drained every night. It seemed hard to believe there'd be time or energy for any of the specialized troopers to start a new relationship. Obviously, Helena didn't have that problem. "Congratulations," Ivy said, recovering with a grin. "Who is the guy?"

"He's a police officer. We met on a case. His name is Everett."

Figured. They could probably relate to each other in a way Ivy never had a chance to with Sean. "I guess that means Luna approves."

Luna looked up at the mention.

"Oh, Ivy." Fiona Duncan, Minnie's daughter and the owner of the B and B, entered the hallway from a side room. "I'm sorry for the intrusion to your sleep last night."

Helena pursed her lips ever so slightly, and Ivy understood the silent message. Fiona didn't know the whole story, so Ivy should keep quiet.

Fiona stopped prematurely when she eyed Luna. The Norwegian elkhound looked fierce when it stared down a person. The innkeeper nodded a greeting at the dog. "We've never had any intruders before. The guests know the troopers prevented an altercation. That's all," she whispered conspiratorially. "And you can be assured that we're updating all our security and check-in protocols. The locks are getting changed today. That nice trooper, Gabriel, helped us see where we can improve."

Fiona spun around, beckoning them. "Follow me. I've got a big breakfast lined up for everyone. We pride ourselves on a family atmosphere. Everyone that stays here is always so friendly and fascinating. They come from all over the world, you know. Bird-watchers, gold hunters, yachters taking a break to check reports on ice before crossing the Northwest Passage… You'd be surprised how many different kinds of folks show up here!"

Helena exchanged an amused grin with Ivy but remained silent. Fiona was full of energy and had never met someone she wasn't able to wring out their life story. Maybe the troopers should consider using her as a confidential informant, as she knew everything and everyone in the Nome area. The woman reached the threshold of the dining room and paused. "See that man the trooper is talking to?" Fiona's voice had dropped back down to her juicy-news whisper that Ivy knew so well. Looking in the direction that the innkeeper indicated, she saw that Gabriel was already in the dining room, shaking hands with a scruffy-looking man among the half a dozen guests already seated at tables.

"Mark Gilles is his name. He's looking to buy some dogs from a husky breeder in the area. He's hoping to start an Iditarod team, training in Anchorage." Fiona's eyebrows waggled. "See what I mean? Fascinating people."

"I saw a loose husky yesterday." She glanced at Helena to confirm that the trooper understood the significance. Could it be the murdered woman had something to do with the man interested in starting a husky team?

"And then those two men in sweaters, Evan Rodgers and Hudson Campbell," Fiona said with a little nod. "They're the ones at the table for two. They've been keeping to themselves, but it's because they came here trying to buy a sizable set of mining claims. Those gold-seeking types try to stay on the down low, but don't you worry." She placed a hand on her heart and spoke so rapidly it was hard to keep up. "My Ben comes from a third-generation gold-mining family. We're giving those men tips to make sure they won't get swindled. Ever since the latest gold rush here, and the host of reality shows, we get all sorts trying to make their fortune."

"There's still active gold mining?" Helena asked.

"Oh, yes! In fact, my Ben built one of the largest working dredges in use today. He can tell you all about it, if you'd like. But be careful who you talk to around here. Everyone acts like they know how to mine gold, but they don't." She straightened. "Well, there's the missing member of your party. I set aside the extra dining room in case you troopers want privacy." She moved into the dining room, arms out in greeting, ready to mingle with her guests.

"I wonder if she's telling her guests about us in kind," Helena mused.

"I don't think she will," Ivy said. "Fiona's

loyal and tight-lipped about locals. She would be about her guests as well if she thought the topic needed privacy." At least, she hoped so.

At the opposite end of the hallway, Sean and Grace approached. She'd always appreciated his dark blond hair, blue eyes and broad shoulders, but now he seemed more rugged, more mature. He was going to be one of those men who only got more attractive with age.

The dog opened her mouth as if in a smile. Helena and Luna followed Fiona into the dining area. The smell of bacon and sausage and freshly brewed coffee beckoned Ivy in farther. Sean accompanied her to the buffet table in the back of the room. "I'd be glad to help you get a plate for Dylan."

"That's very thoughtful, thank you, but—" Dylan reached out his arms and practically vaulted out of hers. Sean easily accepted him and pressed him against his chest. She opened her hands to take him back. "I'm so sorry. He never does that."

"No, it's okay." He grinned down at Dylan. "Make your plates. We've got a little meeting room set aside in back to discuss today's plan. See you in there."

Dylan was busy messing with the badge on Sean's uniform, acting as if he didn't even notice Ivy wasn't with him. For a man who didn't want to have kids, he was frustratingly great with them. She sloppily piled a large plate of food she could share with Dylan and entered the side room where Helena had been watching for her. Helena closed the glass door behind her when she entered. A tablet sat on the center of the table with a live feed of Trooper Maya Rodriguez, if Ivy remembered the team member's name right.

"Not much of an update," Maya said. "We're still on the search to find the groom and best man from the missing-bride case."

Awareness hit Ivy. Months ago, back in April, Sean had called Ivy to ask her a series of questions about survivalists, specifically about the community in residence in Chugach State Park. Unfortunately, she didn't know much about that particular area, but she gave him general tips.

He'd said the park was at the center of two separate cases. First, the missing-bride case that had been all over the news. A wedding party had been in the park when the future bride had become murderous, according to the groom and best man, at least. Then the bride had disappeared, rumored to be pregnant with the groom's baby and hiding somewhere in the state park with survivalists. The second case revolved around helping their team tech, Eli Partridge, search for his god-mother's survivalist relatives in order to relay news of her fight against cancer.

Ivy had been curious to hear updates on both cases. She put down her plates at the edge of the table where she wouldn't be visible in the video feed and took Dylan back from Sean. Thankfully, her sweet boy only had eyes for the dogs and wasn't making too much noise.

"Sorry, this will only take a minute," Sean whispered. "A quick team update."

"I was able to track the groom, Lance Wells, to Anchorage," Trooper Hunter Mc-Cord said. Ivy recognized his voice instantly. "The groom may have been a step ahead of us, but disguises are not his strong suit. Unfortunately, there was some gunfire, and he managed to get away. He won't next time."

The way the trooper spoke, it sounded like the real villain was the groom instead of the missing bride.

"No sign of Jared Dennis, the best man," Maya added. "And I believe Hunter also received news from Ariel Potter, the maid of honor, or maybe I should refer to her as the future Mrs. McCord."

Ivy could see a bit of the screen and Hunter flashed a bashful grin, which seemed out of

place for the man. From the context, it seemed
Hunter and Ariel were an item now.

"Yes," Hunter said. "Ariel received a call
from Violet James. I think it's safe to say she
wouldn't call herself a bride-to-be anymore.
She's grateful that everyone knows she's not
a murderer now, but she's not coming home
until Lance and Jared are behind bars."

Ivy tried not to react, but she knew her
face betrayed her. That was a big update. The
bride was no longer a murder suspect. But the
groom and best man were?

"Violet is too worried they'll find her and
hurt her future baby," Hunter said. "So for
now, she stays hidden. She didn't confirm or
deny that she's found safe harbor with survivalists, but I think it's a good guess."

Sean had his arms crossed over his chest.
"That makes it harder on us to wrap this case
up."

Hunter agreed and the rest of the team
members reported no other news. Helena
tapped on the tablet and the team said their
goodbyes. "Sorry about that. Normally, we
would ask you to wait in another room while
we had the meeting, but circumstances…"

"That's okay." Ivy took a seat. "I'd already
heard about the other case in the news when
Sean asked me about survivalists, so I was

curious to hear updates. I'm sorry I wasn't able to offer more help about the missing survivalists in Chugach State Park."

Gabriel's eyebrows rose. "I'd forgotten we'd had Sean ask you. You're practically a consultant, then," he said, a teasing lilt in his voice, before he took a big bite of an egg sandwich.

"If the groom and the best man are the actual murderers of that tour guide, then I don't blame Violet for staying hidden until you guys catch them." She met Sean's gaze. "I would do anything to protect Dylan. Which is why I'm going to take you back to that shack today and help you catch that killer so he'll leave us alone once and for all."

FIVE

Sean took a deep breath. "If you could give us some landmarks to look for, I think that's all we'll need."

"It would be faster if I showed you," Ivy told him. "Besides, there is the matter of traps."

"Don't worry about that. Gabriel and I have been in this situation before. We sidestepped some nasty traps in Chugach, actually—"

"Barely, but technically that's true," Gabriel added.

Sean tossed a glare his way. His teammate wasn't helping his case. The last thing he wanted was Ivy to be put in danger again, but Gabriel folded his arms over his chest, seemingly nonplussed. "We also had a park ranger give us some tips on how to avoid them."

"And yet your dogs found the traps before you," Ivy said. "Not all the traps are at a dog's level. Did this park ranger give you some hands-on training?" Dylan wiggled in her arms as she studied both of their faces a moment. Sean tried to look confident, but Ivy nodded triumphantly. "That's what I thought. This is what I do, Sean. You know that."

"Of course I do." Before he became a trooper, he'd wanted a little extra wilderness training to prepare himself for the type of remote Alaskan locations he might find himself in. That was why he'd signed up to take a survivalist course all those years ago. Ivy had not only put him through the paces of making shelters and fires no matter the weather or topography, she'd also filled him with confidence that he'd make a great trooper. And here she was, sitting in front of him, more beautiful than the day he'd met her, despite the weariness in her features. If he couldn't keep his own wife—*ex-wife*, he corrected himself again—out of harm's way, then what good was he as a trooper?

"She'll be safer with us, anyway," Gabriel said.

Helena nodded. "Sorry, Sean. Gabriel is right. Why would our suspect return to the shack, knowing that's the first place we would most likely look for him? The guy would have to be bold or stupid to try anything else knowing Ivy has troopers on her right and left."

Sean's memory flickered with recognition. He'd said something similar to Trooper Will Stryker when he'd been trying to keep the woman Will was falling for safe. "I've had my fill of bold and stupid criminals lately."

Gabriel stood and paced the length of the room with Bear at his side. "Agreed, but Ivy also has a point. She's the most qualified to help us investigate the evidence without dogs or troopers getting maimed. If her babysitter is willing to watch Dylan in a new location for the morning, we might get what we need to wrap this case up by nightfall."

Despite his pessimism, hope sputtered to life in his chest. "All right. I give up. If Ivy's willing…"

"You know I am," Ivy murmured, bouncing Dylan on her knee.

The toddler smiled contentedly, then turned around and climbed up her shoulder. "Mama. Doggy." Her face glowed with joy as she kissed his cheek in response.

Sean's insides turned cold. He couldn't really pinpoint exactly why that happened every time she kissed her baby boy.

"Speaking of tracking our suspect down…"

Helena interjected. "Gabriel, did you get the rundown about our guests from Fiona, too?"

Gabriel smirked. "Yes, along with a history of the best and finest visitors ever to grace the shores of the Golden Beaches. I don't believe any of the guests in the dining room are suspects. Bear or Luna would've given us some unusual behavior. Especially Luna if she got her teeth close to the man."

"That's true," Helena said.

Gabriel held up an index finger. "But I'd like to follow up with the man who wants to buy huskies for an Iditarod team. Ask him a few questions and perhaps interview the breeder he's here to see."

"Mark Gilles is his name," Helena said. "And I think that's a good idea."

Sean pondered the new information. "You want to interview him because of the husky Ivy spotted? Sounds like a peripheral lead, but I'm all for turning every stone." He nodded at Gabriel. "So you'll take the interview? I think Helena might be more useful at the shack if Luna really got that close to the suspect."

Helena stood and wiggled her fingers at Dylan. "Let's get this cute little guy somewhere safe with Minnie and hit the road."

Thirty minutes later, Sean drove the Jeep

back in the direction of the shack. A quick glance in the rearview mirror confirmed Helena trailed behind them in the SUV. In the back seat of the Jeep, Grace had settled her head into the now-empty car seat. He wanted to let off a joking warning about not getting too attached to the boy, but he had a feeling the commentary would fall flat. Ivy sat rigid in the passenger seat.

"Hey," he said softly. "You don't have to do this, you know?"

She blinked rapidly and pulled her shoulders back. "I'm actually glad to go back to the scene so soon, with you and Helena. It's like getting back on a horse after you've fallen. This is my home. I can't be scared to be here. I've always loved going until the road ends. Dad would take us to the Niukluk River to fish for fun."

Sean pulled his chin back. "For *fun*? You mean for food?"

"We usually went to the store for food. I mean we needed to know how to catch a fish in the event we needed to, but…" She eyed him. "You might have a different idea of my childhood than the reality of it."

"I'm just a little surprised, I guess. You said you didn't want to raise a child the same way you were raised."

"That was back when I was under the impression you still wanted kids. Just because I don't want to repeat the choices my parents made doesn't mean I didn't learn a lot of valuable things from my childhood. Clearly, there are a lot of things I love about the survivalist way of life or I wouldn't have chosen the occupation I did." Her voice lost the earlier warmth. "Please stop at the mission first. I'd like to pick up some supplies that'll make it easier to spot the traps."

He flipped on the turn signal in advance to give Helena warning. Grace sat up in the back and stared right into the mirror. It seemed like she was shaking her head ever so slightly as if even she knew he'd put his foot in his mouth. He pulled into the gravel parking lot and parked right next to the trooper SUV he'd left in the lot the night before.

"Sean—"

The side door, ajar, waved back and forth in the arctic breeze. There was no way Helena would've left that open. "Stay here."

He stepped out of the Jeep and reached for his holster, with a glance at his colleague. "I see it," Helena said. "I know I locked up before I left. I'll lead with Luna to check it out."

"I'll be your backup." Sean turned around and led Ivy and Grace into his trooper vehicle. "You'll be safer inside here." Though, he hoped they wouldn't need the extra ballistic protection the vehicle offered. "Wait here until I give the all clear." Ivy wrapped her arms around herself and nodded. "Grace, protect." He flipped the locks and closed the door.

Helena waited on the stairs to the deck. He jogged up behind her and they approached with renewed caution. She grabbed the swinging door, keeping it from slamming closed again.

He tapped her on the shoulder. "Let me peek through the windows before you go in." He kept his hand on his weapon as he stepped past the doorway. With an uneasy feeling in his gut, he flattened his back against the small strip of siding in between the doors and windows, then peeked inside. Great. Just as he'd suspected. The store was destroyed. Nothing left on the shelves. Everything scattered on the ground. "Ransacked. No sign of anyone, but I can't see the upstairs apartment."

Helena nodded and shouted inside. "State Troopers! Hands up and exit the building. I'm about to release the dog and she *will* bite you."

They waited, staring at the empty threshold for what seemed like forever. Then he gave the nod. Helena released Luna and the dog tore through the building at breakneck speed. She ran back, panting, the familiar look of disappointment. "No one's here."

"So, was the ransacking a statement? Or was he looking for something?" Helena placed her hands on her hips and stepped inside.

Sean followed her. "Assuming it's the same guy, I think he's after something." His heart pounded harder with the implication. "Ivy said the man demanded to know where something was. He never said what."

"I think it might be helpful to ask her again. She might remember something, a small detail, which could prove invaluable." Helena gingerly moved a backpack on the floor with her foot. Blankets, ropes, packaged food and every other necessity needed in the wild were strewn all over the floor. "We'll also need her to give us an inventory list and a statement. She might notice something missing. Maybe he got what he was looking for. Does she own this place?"

His neck heated. He wasn't 100 percent sure. Ivy had talked a lot about the mission and her life in Nome the last time they'd spoken on the phone, but she'd also never mentioned Dylan. There might be other things she'd held back. "A friend owns this, I believe. Ivy just manages the place and lives here." He nodded toward the stairs. "I want to do one more sweep upstairs before we bring her in."

Helena glanced at Luna but nodded.

"I'm not questioning Luna's skills. She would've let us know a person was here, but I want to make sure he didn't leave some gruesome kind of threat for Ivy anywhere."

Her eyebrows rose. "I'm sorry. I didn't think of that." She nodded to the door. "We'll start the inventory down here while you check."

The stairs creaked as he took the steps two at a time. Entering her living space was surreal. This was where Ivy lived, *without* him. The living room held a love seat with a purple afghan. Sean's lips quirked. She loved purple. The kitchen and dining room were adjacent in the open layout. He passed by the kitchen counter on the way to the two bedrooms. In the center was a stack of papers with a pen to the side. Had he been right? Had the man left a written threat?

His eyes drifted to the top of the sheet. *Adoption Application Letter of Intent.* His fingers rested on the papers. Foster care was one thing…but adoption? His insides churned. No wonder she refused to leave. She wouldn't go anywhere without her soon-to-be son.

He closed his eyes for the briefest of seconds. There was no going back. No trying again. She had a child, and he needed to accept it and shut the door on any what-ifs for their relationship. The only way to do that was to make sure she was safe. The man had gotten careless. They'd catch him, but he needed proof to make the murder charges stick. Ivy's and Helena's voices could be heard from below. Grace sprinted up the stairs to his side. Timely. They had a body to find.

Ivy tightened the paracord to the thin branch she'd found on the dirt road near the river.

"Are you—" Sean began.

"I haven't changed my mind, Sean. Besides, I need something to distract me from the state of the store and my apartment." Truth was her insides still vibrated as intensely as the two other times that man had violated her personal space. First, the kidnapping, then breaking into her room. And now...*this*. It was almost too much. Pawing through all her belongings and vandalizing the mission almost broke her. The back of her neck tingled as if the man was watching her still. She couldn't escape him. Ivy turned her back to Sean so she could squeeze her fists tight without his noticing. It was either that or scream in frustration. "This is the only thing I know to do. I'm also good at tracking."

"I know."

"Please let me do what I can." And if she didn't succeed today, she'd take Dylan to the bunker. Away from the world. Safe. They'd stay there as long as it took.

"So what's the plan?" Helena approached her with Luna at her side.

"I walk forward with this stick outstretched. The cord is weighted just enough to hang straight down but light enough it won't trigger any trip wires. We should be able to see if it catches on anything before we step into danger."

Sean reached out his hand. "I'll hold it, then." She opened her mouth to argue, but his eyes narrowed. "Ivy, I draw the line at you going into the trees first. Besides, you'll probably be able to notice faster if you're not the one holding the paracord." He offered Grace's leash. "Trade?" At her resigned nod, he glanced at Grace. "Heel. Ivy." He pointed.

Grace shuffled backward, her spine straight and her head perfectly aligned with Ivy's left foot. "I didn't think she'd be willing to work with anyone but you."

"She won't. She knows you, so I think she

understands what I'm asking. Even without the leash, I'd expect her to remain in a heel with you until I release her." He tilted his head with a smile. "She's the best partner I've ever had."

Luna huffed behind them, prompting Helena to laugh. "No need for jealousy, Luna. You're the best partner I've ever had, too."

Sean turned around and held his arm straight. The stick added a good four to five feet from his arm and the cord dangled just as Ivy had hoped. "Stay behind and be my eyes." He took a deep breath and squared his shoulders. "Here we go."

Ivy's heart rate sped up. Grace leaned against her leg for the briefest of moments. Was she trying to comfort her? Ivy fought against blinking, watching the string and scanning the environment for potential setups. There. The tip of the branch on the right tree hung down in a curve. *"Stop!"*

Despite it still being daylight, she'd found a flashlight on the floor of her shop and brought it along. She flipped it on and pointed its light at a branch. The beam produced a reflection off a thin filament. And while the line might seem like a spiderweb to most, she knew better. "Stay put a second." She dropped the leash, and Sean commanded Grace to stay.

With a flick of her knife, she cut the line and located the spikes, hidden in the tall grasses, set to be used as projectiles. "Hopefully, the cord would've caught it, but if I can spot them before we get that far, even better. You were right. If I'm not holding the cord, I can see more."

She hated admitting her failures and weaknesses to Sean, no matter how small. Their divorce was like a giant F on her report card in marriage. He seemed to have changed in many ways. The old Sean would've stubbornly refused her help, even with her expert qualifications, and she would've defiantly refused his.

He seemed more thoughtful now, too, but maybe that was just because he was on the job. He brought his best to work. She always knew that. And besides, she was becoming a mom, so she really needed to stop caring what he thought of her.

She picked the leash back up and took a step forward, but Grace didn't budge. Sean grinned. "Heel to Ivy." The journey through the thick grasses was slow going. A few yards later, Grace whined before the dangling paracord had caught on anything.

"I think this is the trap she found last time," he said.

Grace made a noise two other times, the paracord revealed three more traps, and Ivy found another right before they reached a small clearing by the river. "There." She pointed. Through another set of trees, the shack blended in with the surrounding brush.

Her insides twisted, but she took a deep breath and looked around, wondering if the husky was still in the area. No movement, except the slight breeze. Her heartbeat pounded against her throat. She might miss something if she didn't get a grip. "I need you and Helena to keep an eye out, too, now," she told Sean. "There's a lot to watch for."

She spotted another set of traps identical to the log smasher she'd found the day she escaped. Luna helped Helena find a ground trap, and finally they made it to the front door of the shack. Sean reached around her for the handle.

Something didn't seem right. Ivy blocked his hand. "Not yet."

Grace whined and Sean raised an eyebrow. "It's best not to make contact with me like that. Grace might feel forced to choose her loyalty. She doesn't give a warning if she feels she needs to protect me."

Irritation coursed through her veins, but she didn't have time to examine why. Grace wasn't a pet, after all—she was Sean's partner—but she'd be lying if she said she didn't love the dog. "I had good reason. If the murderer takes the time to set traps, he's probably smart enough to know I'd bring you guys back here."

"Fair point," Helena said.

Ivy flipped on the flashlight and guided the beam along the peripheral of the door. Parallel to the doorknob there was the slightest change, but it could be simply part of the construction. "Might be light reflecting off the latch," she muttered before moving the beam around the outer perimeter. Grace whined again. "I can't see anything but—"

Luna also complained. "Okay, it's time to trust our instincts. Something definitely feels off," Helena said. "Maybe our guy really is still inside there."

"Stand back," Sean said, looking around for any potential projectile trap. "Put Luna on ready alert."

Helena guided Ivy and Grace to the side they'd already cleared of traps. They could see the door but were far enough away to miss any projectiles. "Ready," Helena declared both to Luna and Sean.

He moved to the opposite side of the doorknob and crouched down against the shack wall. "State Troopers!" He reached across the door and turned the knob until a click. He leaned back and used the stick with the paracord to shove the door wide open.

A gunshot rang out. The dogs barked and lunged forward, straining against the leashes. A cloud of dirt and Sean's prone body were all Ivy could see.

SIX

"State Troopers," Helena shouted, a slight tremble in her voice that only other troopers would be able to detect. "You have five seconds to leave the premises with your hands up or I send the dog in and she will bite. Five…"

"I'm fine," Sean yelled back. "He missed me." The jolt of hearing a shotgun at close range made him lose his balance and fall back. He was more on edge than he'd thought after discovering so many traps, but now they were going to get this guy. He popped back up on his feet, pressed his back against the wall and grabbed his weapon out of its holster. Helena's counting grew stronger, steadier.

"One." She took a deep breath as the threshold of the shack door remained empty. "Attack!"

Sean stepped inside immediately after Luna, his weapon raised. Helena stepped to the right. The shack was empty except for the

gun, an old spring-loaded twenty-gauge shotgun rigged up to shoot in the corner. The K-9
still stood on guard, staring at the shotgun,
while Helena sliced at the rig used to engage
the trigger with the door's motion.

Sean moved cautiously in case there was
another trap. His eyes roamed the interior,
taking note of the rotting wooden roof, the
structural beam, the ropes on the ground, the
blood on the floor... His throat went dry.

"He knew we'd come back," Helena said.

"He meant to kill." Ivy stood at the door,
her features unnaturally blank as she scanned
the room. Grace passed her and stepped into
the room, spinning and then sniffing the floor
in front of him. Grace sat down and looked
directly at Sean. A thick layer of dust formed
a border, a perfect rectangle, around the K-9.

"Did she just alert?" Helena asked softly.

Sean didn't want to discuss it in Ivy's presence, but he nodded. Even if the body wasn't
actively in the room, the cadaver dog would
be able to smell death for up to two weeks,
though never past a month. While it probably seemed rare to Helena for Grace to alert
without prompting, they thankfully weren't
accosted with the scent of recent death all
the time.

He wanted Ivy out of here as fast as possible. He pointed at the border of dust around his K-9 partner. "A rug was here?"

She nodded but said nothing.

Helena placed a hand on Ivy's shoulder. "Are you okay? You don't have to stay in here."

"I'm fine." But her voice sounded barely over a whisper. "When I woke up, the man had already rolled the rug up." She pointed to where Grace still sat. "I didn't see the woman inside, but I… I saw a hand." Her eyes drifted to the pole behind Sean and her entire face went white. "Excuse me. The dust must be getting to me." She spun on her heel and stepped back outside.

Seeing where the man had kept her, what he had put her through, what could've happened… For a moment, he heard nothing but roaring in his ears until Helena stared him down.

"Did you hear me? I said she's safe now."

"I know."

Helena pulled out her phone and began taking photographs of the shotgun and of Grace sitting on the only clean portion of the floor, along with images of the ropes on the ground. Sean rewarded the K-9 with her favorite toy. Afterward, he walked out of the shack with Grace by his side to where Ivy waited, her arms wrapped around herself, staring toward the river.

Was she *really* safe?

"See that riverbank?" Ivy murmured. "That's where I saw him without his mask."

He didn't need her to repeat the description. The words were burned into his memory. Six foot three with auburn hair and pale skin. He hesitated, but he had to do it. "Do you remember any other details now?"

She shook her head. "If that husky hadn't distracted him..."

"We would've found you in time," Sean finished for her, an edge to his voice that he knew probably wasn't helpful. Every fiber of his being told him to pull her close, to tell her he was so thankful she was okay. But he couldn't. For so many reasons.

They stood together in silence for two minutes. Sean placed a hand on her shoulder, ever so gently. He couldn't stand to see her like this. Ivy turned into his touch and tilted her head, wordlessly studying him. She stepped closer, and it was like two magnets coming together. He wrapped his arms around her, ignoring the warning bells in his mind. Her hands gripped the back of his jacket, the comfort of her touch no match for the many layers. He missed being able to hold her this way.

The feeling that nothing could topple them if they were together, leaning on each other. He had no right to think of them this way.

Sean abruptly stepped back. Grace dropped the toy at his feet, and he picked it up. "Grace, it's time to work. Lead."

The extra word meant everything to the K-9. It was her cue that she was to take him to the body she'd smelled in the shack. Her ears swiveled and her spine straightened, her nose straining forward. He had to focus on the case now. At least they'd already passed by this section and knew it was free from traps. Still, he didn't want to take any chances and kept his eyes trained for any potential areas traps may be hiding. He knew from the way Ivy followed his exact steps that she was doing the same.

Grace kept her nose down to the ground. A line in the dirt, roughly six inches wide and headed straight, indicated she was likely on the right track. Helena and Luna joined them, a few paces behind. "The river?" his colleague asked.

"He might've taken the body to a different location with the boat," Sean answered. "We heard a motor moments after we found Ivy. He could've changed his plan after her escape and gone far from here. I'm hoping Grace can lead us in the right direction."

"A metallic fishing boat," Ivy said. "That's what he put the rug in. I remember that much. It looked old and beat-up."

"That's good," Helena praised her. "Feel free to tell us anything from that day, even if you think it might not matter. Every detail has the potential to help."

Sean studied Grace as she paused, lifting her head. *Come on, Lord. Please help her tell us which way he took her next.* The dog turned in a full circle, her mouth hanging open, breathing in the air. She returned to the waterline and plunged her face into the river. Her head jerked back. She shook, water droplets flying from her ears and neck, but even after, she didn't sit. If she had sat, they would've called in divers and searched the bottom of the river. Sean knew they still might have to resort to that, but given the amount of tributaries, he didn't like the options. Besides, the riverbed seemed to get shallow in places with rocks jutting out and tree roots sticking out from the bank. Grace huffed and looked over her shoulder. Her eyes grew soft, and by the way she held her head, he knew she was disappointed. He patted his leg. "Good job." Her tail wagged in acknowledgment.

"Dead end?" Helena asked.

Sean hated that phrase in his specialty, even

if it described the truth. "The trail is cold."
As well as his hope that he'd be able to close
the case anytime soon. He was going to have
to beg for more resources that weren't there.
Someone would need to take over in keeping
Ivy safe because he and Grace would need
to systematically comb every square inch of
Alaskan tundra until they found the victim.
The colonel might not understand, but Sean
would have to *make* her understand. Ivy was
one of their own. Well, she used to be. Begging may not buy him much time, but he'd be
willing to take unpaid leave and keep going.
If he discovered a body while he wasn't on
duty, the corpse would still be evidence.

The clock was ticking. The longer they
waited, the more chance the suspect got away
with getting rid of the body. Sean couldn't
live with himself if the killer succeeded.

Ivy missed her Jeep. The seats in the state
trooper SUV weren't the most comfortable.
"Do you often have to leave your car in Anchorage and use other troopers' vehicles?"

"Uh, not usually. Typically, I can drive to
where I need to go." He followed behind Helena on the highway. They ascended a hill next
to the sea. Movement in the peripheral caught
her eye.

"What—" Sean's mouth hung open as he slammed on the brakes.

A massive herd of caribou—almost fifty, if she had to guess—ran into the road from the eastern tundra. A sea of brown in front of them made it hard to distinguish where one animal ended and another began. Their antlers held the answer to how many were in the herd, but at the moment, they were so close together, it would be impossible to count.

The radio squawked. "You guys okay?" Helena asked. "I've never seen so many reindeer at once!" She'd been far enough ahead that the herd hadn't blocked her path.

"Should I tell her they're called caribou around here?" Ivy whispered to Sean.

"They're not reindeer?"

"Same animal, believe it or not. But if they're wild, they're technically called caribou. If they're domesticated, then they're called reindeer. People will know what you mean either way, but they might school you."

"Like you just did?" Sean winked and grabbed the radio. "We're fine, but the *caribou*," he emphasized, "don't appear in a hurry to go anywhere." He tested the horn and the herd jogged a few steps forward but then stopped again.

"I'll wait a few minutes," Helena said.

Ivy leaned her head back, trying to calm the butterflies in her stomach. All from something as innocent as Sean's wink. How often had that wink been used after a meal or a funny joke? It was an invitation to get closer, to snuggle up. It didn't mean that anymore. Just like that hug at the river didn't mean anything. Two people simply trying to get past thoughts of a horrible crime. That was all it signified. A few of the caribou turned, watching them. "I think they're used to vehicles and aren't too scared of them."

"Why not?" Sean leaned forward, his arms draped on top of the steering wheel. "Why are they in the road? And why all *guys*?"

Ivy laughed. "Both males and females have antlers when it comes to reindeer."

"Don't you mean caribou?" he teased.

"Same thing," she said in a deadpan, though she ended up smiling a second later. "And, to answer your question, this is actually common around here. When the road isn't covered in snow or water, it's easier for them to travel on than the tundra. You'll find lots of animal herds prefer to travel by road. Or—" she squinted into the distance, searching for any other animals "—they could be running from a grizzly."

"I have bear spray, but nothing to encourage caribou to move on. Not sure I'd want to anger anyone with antlers."

He grabbed his radio. "Think I should tell Katie where she can find more reindeer?"

Helena responded instantly. "Probably wouldn't be appreciated. Besides, her ranch only helps injured, orphaned or unwanted ones. These all look fine to me. If you don't want me to wait for you, I'll start processing the crime scene photos and meet you at the trooper headquarters."

"That's affirmative. See you soon." Sean clicked the radio off.

"Are you talking about the receptionist, Katie?" Ivy asked. "Why would she want to find reindeer?"

"She's actually the team director's assistant."

Ivy vaguely remembered the green-eyed petite young woman. Always businesslike and professional, even at team gatherings. "Katie Kapowski?"

"That's the one. Turns out her aunt Addie owns The Family K Reindeer Ranch Sanctuary. It's a mouthful. Like Helena was saying, it operates more like a rescue center for reindeer. I found the whole thing a little confusing when I see them out here in the wild, but your explanation makes sense. Maybe they aren't technically wild anymore. They've been abandoned or—"

"—lost their herd?"

"I'm sure Katie would know. It's been on the team's radar because lately someone has been stealing the reindeer."

"Why would anyone do that?" Ivy tried to focus on the good in the world, but this week seemed to be relentless in showing her the worst of humanity.

"That's one of many questions we have. She thought her aunt was her only living relative, but we've discovered an estranged uncle, Terrence Kapowski. Her aunt Addie hadn't acknowledged his existence to Katie until recently."

"Oh, wow. That's unexpected. Have they reunited?"

He raised his eyebrows. "Gabriel has actually been trying to locate him. Before he was called here, he'd been tracking Terrence's whereabouts near the ranch. A bunch of the locals recognized his photo, so we can place him nearby. Bringing him in for questioning has just become a high priority for the team."

"But why would Katie's uncle target the reindeer ranch? Why not reach out and try to make amends? Do you know why he was estranged?"

He glanced at her. "You're asking all the right questions. Miss shoptalk?"

She felt her cheeks heat. "More like I'm curious what makes people tick. I deal with all sorts who come to the mission, ready to try out the survivalist way of life." She did miss hearing about what was happening in the team's lives, though. Learning about cases like the reindeer ranch felt like a small connection to the old "how was your day?" chats they used to have at dinners.

"The team doesn't know the answers to any of your questions yet. Terrence, the estranged uncle, never showed at the funeral of his mom and dad. They passed away almost a decade ago. So we're working with the theory that maybe he just now found out that he wasn't included in the will. He could be lashing out."

"Katie's aunt inherited the reindeer sanctuary?"

"Sole inheritance. Though, none of us understands what Terrence hopes to accomplish by stealing orphaned reindeer. As soon as Gabriel gets back to Anchorage, he's going to take Bear and track the man down. Then hopefully we'll have some answers. Oh, look! They're moving." Sean rolled slowly after the herd, as they picked up speed down the road, and took a sharp right into a field.

"It struck me that I'd never seen your job in action before today."

He whipped his head in her direction, his eyebrows raised.

"Training, yes," she clarified, "but not working."

His shoulders sagged. "It can be draining, but I know what I do is important."

"I've always known that," she said softly. She truly had. Standing on that riverbank, she'd found herself hoping he and Grace would locate the victim, ensuring they'd have enough evidence to capture the murderer and lock him away forever. How many people had Sean's work brought justice and closure to? She'd never asked him, partly because he liked to leave his cases behind when he came home.

But after months of seeing him drained, she got aggravated. Day after day, promises unkept. Promises he probably shouldn't have ever made before he knew what the job would demand of him. Promises she maybe should've released him from.

The thought smacked her over the head. Was she softening toward him? Perhaps. She twisted her lips to the side. Her tenderhearted feelings toward Sean were natural, though, since they'd been a couple for so long. And it didn't mean she wanted to be back together with him…

In her foster parenting classes, she'd been learning about attachment hormones. They amplified senses and memories to ensure a parent and child bonded. Like the way she smelled Dylan's head and adored the clean shampoo scent from his hair before she laid him down for the night. There was probably something similar between exes. Which meant she should probably disregard the confusing feelings for him without a second's hesitation.

At least, she *hoped* that was the case…

"I'm sorry about all this," Sean said, nodding toward the mission as they passed by. "As soon as the investigation is wrapped up, I can help you tidy up inside." Another state trooper vehicle sat in the parking lot, a trooper she didn't recognize walking around the perimeter of the building.

After the excitement at the shack, she'd almost forgotten about the break-in. "Not your fault." She looked past Sean to the Bering Sea churning next to the highway. A spray of water shot up in the air. Likely beluga whales this time of year.

"When you moved out, I'd hoped that away from me you'd at least be safe." He blanched and pressed his lips together, as if he hadn't meant to say anything.

She blinked rapidly. Had he really worried about her while they were in Anchorage? "Safety was never our problem, was it?"

He shrugged, which seemed odd. Almost as if he thought that maybe it *was* part of their issues. That made no sense, though. They never had disagreements surrounding her safety.

She would head to the bunker tonight. The possibility that the man wouldn't stop trying to hunt her down was foremost in her mind, but she didn't have the emotional bandwidth to deal with any more today. Maybe tomorrow. Tonight, she would pretend she was on vacation with Dylan in the bunker, far away from even the hints of civilization. She'd refuse to think about anything else except enjoying her sweet little boy's company.

The ocean view disappeared as they rolled past houses and the downtown with the fake Western awnings, heading to where Minnie was watching Dylan. To the right, the largest parking lot in town was dedicated to portable gold dredges. The dredges were designed for the ocean, set on boats. The vessels had to be large enough to hold machinery to dig up the seafloor, carry it to filters and spit back the remaining dirt into the water, sans rock and gold. The boat on wheels closest to them stretched out almost two hundred feet and likely belonged to Minnie's family. The expense to rent or own a parking lot of this size must be high. A chain stretched from the tip of the boat to the ground and was attached to a husky's collar.

"Stop!" She pointed in the dog's direction.

Sean slammed on the brakes. The seat belt caught her momentum as she tipped forward and back. "What'd you see? Is it him?" Sean asked, eyes roaming the parking lot.

"It's the husky."

He frowned as Grace let out what sounded like a dissatisfied grunt. "Are you sure it's the same husky?" Sean asked.

"Around here, it's unusual to only have one. People always own more than one, and they're never chained up." She tapped the glass window. "Besides, it's a Siberian husky with a gray topcoat that ends with a widow's peak right about the eyes. It's the same dog, Sean."

He reached the radio and called for backup. The dog's attention swiveled their way as he spoke. She wasn't sure the husky could see her face through the tinted windows, but she held her stare. "Maybe the man tied her up and left her. I think she was the victim's dog, not his."

"For all we know, the victim and the suspect were a couple."

What a horrible thought. They sat in tense silence for a few minutes. After just one day, Ivy was already sick of the fear that gripped her heart with every thought of that man.

The side mirror revealed Helena and Gabriel pulling up right behind them, forming a V-shaped barrier from the exit of the parking lot to the road.

"That was fast."

Sean opened his car door and placed a hand on his holster. "They're the best team there is."

It was a good thing the town wasn't busy right now, though they were at the outskirts, far from other houses. At the other end of the parking lot was an alley in between two tall buildings. She had no idea if actual businesses still occupied them. The other two SUVs flashed their lights without sirens.

Sean stepped to the back and released Grace to join him. Ivy opened her side and climbed out. "I'll see to the husky while you three check the area."

"Not yet, Ivy." His hands rose up. "Stay in the—"

Gunshots rang out. Asphalt kicked up at her feet.

SEVEN

Sean ran around the back of the vehicle, but Grace beat him to Ivy. The dog lunged in front of her, ready to protect and take the hit for her. She screamed and covered her head but appeared frozen. Sean wrapped his left arm around Ivy's waist, pulling her backward as another round of bullets fired in their direction. Grace hopped backward, the last shot barely missing her.

Every nanosecond counted when dealing with a shooter. The bullet could hit her or Grace at any moment. He flung open the back door and pulled Ivy behind the glass window. His whistle alerted Grace to follow them to safety. A bullet pinged the glass. The bullet-proof protection held as more rounds were fired. Ivy turned and crawled into the back seat. Grace hopped in beside her. Sean remained hunkered down behind the open door.

Gabriel could be heard over the radio. "Requesting backup. Active shooter. At the edge of Nugget Alley and—"

Another round of bullets. Sirens pierced the air. The Nome police had to be on their way. Confident the open door served as a shield, he shifted to make sure Ivy wasn't hurt. Her arms and legs trembled.

"I'm sorry I got out, Sean."

She shouldn't have to worry about whether or not to get out of a vehicle. He knew her heart. The poor husky, who was now huddled underneath a long extension of the barge, had been her focus. "It's not your fault. Stay here while I take care of this guy." He grabbed his radio. "Anyone get a visual on the shooter?"

Ivy leaned forward, her arm grazing over his shoulder. "Sean, look! Straight through the window. To the right. I saw his red hair."

On the backside of the farthest dredge, closest to the alley, he caught sight of him as well before the head disappeared again. The bullets had stopped. The guy must be running for it. Sean clicked the radio. "At my seven o'clock. Any sign?"

"I thought I saw an elbow. There might be a ladder on the other side of that dredge. I'm switching to speaker," Helena said. She meant that she was about to turn the SUV's radio into a megaphone. "State Troopers!

Drop your weapon and present yourself with hands up in five seconds or we will send the dog and she will bite."

A man leaped off the backside of the dredge, dropping to the ground from a good ten feet up. His hair was no longer visible, a ski mask covering his head. The Nome PD pulled up behind his vehicle, lights flashing but sirens off. The suspect straightened and pumped his arms and legs in a sprint, heading for the alley between the two buildings. Sean groaned inwardly. Why'd they always have to run?

"You'll be safe with the police here. Grace, protect Ivy." He hated to leave his partner behind when he might need her, but she'd serve him best by protecting the woman he— No, he wouldn't let feelings get in the mix at a time like this.

"Attack!" Helena yelled loud enough to be heard without a radio. Luna shot off like a rocket. Sean stepped out from his position of safety, then took off in a sprint right after the dog. Helena's feet rapidly hitting the pavement behind him spurred him on. He pressed harder, faster. Luna was mere feet from snatching the man. Once she grabbed on, they'd have him. The nightmare was about to be over.

The man reached the shadowed alley. Sean moved his hand tentatively to his waist but kept running. He'd only draw his weapon if fired upon. Luna was almost there. Sean had maybe a hundred feet to go. Luna had twenty.

"Freeze!" Sean yelled, expecting any second for Luna to leap and clutch the gunman's right arm.

The man spun to face them, only his eyes and mouth visible through the cutouts of the mask. Sean unlocked his holster to pull his weapon. The man lifted something resembling a shiny glass bauble—as if that'd stop Luna—and threw it down on the ground. Glass shattered before them. Smoke filled the spot in front of the man, obscuring Sean's view.

Luna skittered to a stop just before entering the alley. Sean darted to the far right, lest the gunman could still see him and take aim. What was going on? Luna never hesitated to run through danger. Then the horrific smell hit him. Like rotten eggs and ammonia, except concentrated. An involuntary cough racked his lungs, and he hovered in a squat, trying to hack up the rest of the irritation.

"Luna," Helena choked out. She also hit her knees, coughing.

Because they'd been running at a full

steam, they couldn't help but inhale deeply, only to breathe in more irritants. The sound of a metal door closing echoed from within the alley.

"Step away. Walk with your arms up. That will get fresh air in faster. And get Luna out of there." Gabriel had caught up behind them with Bear. He clicked the radio on his shoulder. "We need immediate backup on other side of alley. Suspect is armed, wearing a ski mask. Over." The smoke had dissipated, but the man hadn't waited around in the long alley. Gabriel pointed at Luna. "If I had to guess, I'd say it's a homemade stink bomb. Hydrogen sulfide and ammonia are toxic together, but only dangerous in extreme amounts."

Sean accepted his analysis without question. His teammate had a broader education in scent work, given Bear's specialty.

"Which means?" Helena asked.

"Luna is safe to keep going as soon as she's ready." Gabriel leaned over just as Bear sneezed, and he offered his K-9 a scent cone. "The smoke bomb will only mess up their scent-tracking momentarily. Now that he's had a good sneeze, Bear's senses are going to be stronger than ever. Let's get this guy."

Sean didn't need to be told twice. He ran

through the alley, hand on his weapon. The smell still hung in the air. A nondescript metal door on the left building wasn't fully closed. He pulled at the handle, and it opened easily into a hallway. *"State Troopers!"* he yelled. His voice echoed off the cinder-block walls.

Gabriel, Bear, Helena and Luna stepped behind him. The building held the musty smell of being abandoned. They froze for a moment, all straining to hear any sounds that might lead them in the right direction. Bear put his nose to the ground for a moment. His head popped up and his tail rose higher. Gabriel nodded. "He's found something." They ran after the dogs. So far, every room they'd passed had been empty.

Bear turned to the right. Gabriel nodded. "Looks like the suspect hit the stairs."

Helena grabbed the stairway door and looked at Luna. "Feel well enough to get to work again, girl?" The dog wagged her tail in response. Unfortunately, they needed to make good and sure the building was actually empty before telling Luna to attack.

She sprinted up the stairs with her partner at her side. Once again, Sean was right behind Luna. If another smoke bomb was lobbed at them, he knew this time it wouldn't hurt him.

The dogs might not be able to run through, but he wouldn't let the smoke stop him.

Except all the doors to the four landing areas were closed. Luna ran to the top of the building stairs and back again to the second floor, where Bear was still sniffing his way up the stairs. The Saint Bernard lifted his head again and pointed to the door. "He's down this hallway," Gabriel said.

Sean kicked at the door until it flung open. Luna charged like she'd been racing on slick floors her entire life. The dog knew what she was after but wouldn't attack until given the word. Helena and Sean ran after her at full speed.

He'd be lying to say he didn't want to be the one to bring the guy in, but the important thing was getting him. Luna darted in and out of each room, so far with no success. Years' worth of dust and grime layered on the windows provided very little light streaming into the building. The back of his neck tingled with the possibility that maybe the man would be able to hide in a darkened corner. Bear, though, was still on the trail, albeit behind them. His sneeze echoed down the hallway, the second time in the last five minutes.

"Dust holds the smell. Don't worry," Gabriel said, his eyes focused on the K-9.

Luna ran up and down the hallway a second time, darting into every single open room, frustration evident by her whine. Helena said the word for her to relax and praised her for the try.

"No." Sean shook his head. "He's got to be here. Bear smelled him. Let's start taking down the closed doors."

"Judging by the names on the doors, this used to be an old mining company," Gabriel said. "They must have had a lot of claims to manage back in the day."

Bear alerted on a closed door on the right. Sean and Gabriel stood on either side of the door. Helena grabbed her Taser while Gabriel and Sean kept their hands on the handles of their guns. She would attempt to detain the suspect peacefully with the help of Luna, but if the man aimed a gun, they would be forced to shoot. Bear stood behind Gabriel, and Sean ticked his fingers off silently. *One, two, three...*

Sean twisted in front of the door and kicked it open. Helena yelled, *"Attack!"*

Gabriel and Sean charged after Luna, instantly moving to opposite sides of the room to leave Helena space. The breeze hit Sean fully in the face. Luna rushed for the open window and dived through it, paws first, disappearing from view.

"No!" Helena yelled.

Sean gasped at the sight. The dog had jumped clean out the window. They raced forward, Helena leaning her torso over the window first. "She's okay!" Sean peered over her shoulder to find Luna on the third stair, descending a rickety steel fire escape. *"Stop, Luna."* The dog froze at Helena's command and looked up. The suspect was nowhere to be seen.

Sirens blared from below. A local Nome police cruiser sped down the street. As the vehicle passed by the building, Sean spotted the source of the chase. At the end of the street, an ATV vaulted over the curb and hopped over rough hills in the tundra. The cruiser screeched to a stop. An officer hopped out of the vehicle and sprinted after him on foot, shouting.

"The suspect is too far away now," Gabriel said. "No more roads out there."

The ATV kept bouncing up and over hills, the light from the headlights appearing dimmer and smaller. The officer stopped after about thirty feet of running and turned to return back to the cruiser.

"What about planes?" Sean asked. "Do we

have a pilot back in the area? What about a certified drone operator?"

"I'll check, but I think the only ones that have those qualifications are still out on assignment," Helena said. She patted the side of her leg and Luna jumped back through the window. She walked off, clicking the radio and asking questions of the Nome PD to see if they had any new leads.

Sean felt paralyzed, squinting in the distance. The man who was determined to kill Ivy had slipped through his fingers once again.

Ivy couldn't keep her eyes off the alley the team had disappeared into, especially after seeing them run past a cloud of smoke. Whatever was happening, Sean was in danger. Was this a normal day's work for him? Had it *always* been?

The Nome police officer blocked her view now, pacing back and forth in the parking lot while speaking into his radio and holding it up to his ear to hear the replies. He'd made the mistake of getting too close to Sean's vehicle to ask Ivy if she needed medical care. Grace had stuck her face up to the window and released a warbled bark that almost sounded like, *Back off, buddy*. It startled the officer enough that he straightened and kept an eye on her from a distance. If Sean didn't return soon, she didn't know who Grace would allow to get near.

Something caught the cop's eye and he turned sideways enough that Ivy could see past him to the three team members with Luna and Bear striding back together. Their shoulders hunched, their heads bent—looking down at the ground as they walked—instead of their usual jovial banter. They appeared weary. Which meant it was doubtful they'd already handed off a handcuffed murderer to the local cops. "I don't think they have good news for us, Grace."

A moment later, Sean beckoned her out of the car with a wave. She pushed open the unlocked door and Grace trotted to Sean's side. "Are you okay?" he asked.

Physically, yes. Emotionally, her insides were vibrating so hard she was going to come unglued. She fought against crying at his question. When the bullets had been firing, she hadn't been able to think clearly. For all her training in survival, her brain had simply switched to panic mode. She looked up to the gray clouds gathering above her. "Unharmed," she said simply.

Only then did she notice Sean seemed to

be avoiding eye contact, as well. After having known each other so fully, she was taken off guard at how vulnerable she still felt in his presence. Like if they looked at each other too long, they might see everything they were trying so hard not to say. Maybe he felt the same way? That seemed unlikely. Sean had always told her he was a simple man. Sure, he'd said it most often when they were trying to figure out what to have for dinner, but he wasn't one to gush.

"He got away, but you probably already figured that," Sean said. "I know you're eager to get Dylan. I'll need to do a sweep of the area with Grace and then we can go."

"With Grace? You think he might've hidden the victim here?" She didn't bother to camouflage the surprise in her tone. Why would the man drag a deceased woman all the way to the shack only to bring her back to town to hide the body? Unless he had a new motive to frame someone.

"It's precautionary," Sean said. "In case he's murdered someone else while here."

Her jaw dropped. She wouldn't have thought of that, though she'd heard that murderers found it easier to kill after the first time. An involuntary shudder worked up her spine. She quickly hugged herself, hoping Sean missed it.

"I hope that won't be the case, but we need to be sure." His eyes connected with hers. "I'm sorry." Maybe she was right to fear he'd see more in her, because his apology wasn't about not catching the guy. What exactly was he trying to say? He frowned and cleared his throat, and the moment was gone. "Grace and I won't be long. You can either stay with us or wait with Helena or Gabriel."

"I'd feel safer with you." The thought slipped out before she could filter it with less emotion.

His eyebrows jumped, but he nodded and turned around. "Time to get to work."

Grace's spine straightened and her tail curled over her back. The transformation from normal dog to working partner always amazed her.

Gabriel and Bear also sniffed each dredge from the parking lot. "Helena is working on finding out who the owners are. We'll start by asking their permission to search these—with warrants, if necessary. Grace shouldn't need to get on the boats to let me know she smells something inside."

His radio came to life. "Bear confirmed the man has recently been in the two largest dredges in the lot but none of the others," Gabriel said.

Sean clicked the button. "So far Grace hasn't alerted on anything."

The moment they got close to the still-chained husky, Ivy ran forward. She'd been dying to check on her condition. The two-toned fur seemed matted compared to yesterday and her striking blue eyes had a hollow, lifeless stare. Her ears flattened, though, and she let Ivy approach with only one warbled bark.

"She's stressed or anxious, huh?" Sean asked. "That's usually when the colonel's dog—also a Siberian husky—talks the most."

Ivy gingerly touched the dog's fur, watching for any signs that it might attack. So far, the dog was docile. Except her fingers touched something dried yet sticky. Her fingers pulled back the husky's thick coat. "There's blood."

Ten minutes later, Ivy paced the vet's lobby while Sean and Grace sat at ease in the chairs. She wanted to know if the husky was okay but simultaneously couldn't wait to get to Dylan. The vet entered from a door labeled Employees Only, and Ivy caught a glimpse of a tech loving on the husky. Her shoulders relaxed slightly. The dog was in good hands.

The vet appeared to be in his late forties with thick dark hair. "I collected the sample of blood. Likely a day old and not from any injury to the dog."

Ivy's head spun. Not from the dog? Could it be from his owner?

"Should I send the sample to the state troopers?"

"That'd be great," Sean said. "Any chip? Any identification of the dog's owner?"

"None, I'm afraid." The vet turned from Sean to Ivy. "I think she'll be fine, but she's underweight and very dehydrated. I'd like to keep her overnight for observation while I run a few tests. As long as she's healthy, I can release her to you tomorrow."

Ivy placed a hand on her chest. "To me?"

"Yes, since you brought her in. I know of no other owner. If you have no interest, animal control will be called. I have to warn you, though—they've been full and have been transferring stray dogs to Anchorage."

Her heart ached at the thought of the sweet animal getting shipped off. She hesitated. "Can I think about it? It's a big decision."

"Of course. Let's touch base tomorrow."

Sean clenched his jaw, clearly trying not to make a face. Ivy ignored the apparent disapproval and smiled at the vet. "Thank you."

They silently returned to the SUV. Grace turned and looked back at the building, as if she was concerned for the husky, as well. Inside the vehicle, Sean's expression remained stony.

She sighed. "I take it you're not happy I'm considering taking home the husky."

"Ivy, I know I don't have a right to make my opinion heard unless it directly pertains to this case." He shrugged. "That said, I can't help that it's still my instinct to keep your best interest in mind. So, if you want my opinion, I trust you'll ask for it. Right now, though, I'm guessing you want to pick up Dylan?"

Her mouth dropped open. It was a lovely speech, but she didn't believe it. What she wanted was to ask him how deciding a year into their marriage, unilaterally, that they wouldn't have kids could be in her *best interest*, but she knew that would only stir up the past and start a fight. "Yes, I'd like to go to Dylan," she said instead.

He'd made it clear he was trying to keep professional boundaries, and yet Ivy's curiosity would not be tamed. "Fine. I'm asking your opinion," she said, before she could change her mind.

He glanced at her, wide-eyed, before composing his features and returning his attention to the road. "It might be nice if you were no longer in danger before deciding to adopt a dog. I mean, you're committing to a forever home, right? In fact, I would think *all* major decisions would be off the table right now, considering that."

"Which is why I said I needed some time to think about it." She reflected on his words again. "But what do you mean by *all* decisions?" Her eyes narrowed. Did he know about the adoption? He'd come down the stairs when she was counting inventory at the mission, too distracted by the destruction of all the displays to have realized the implication. He'd been in her apartment. Had he seen Dylan's adoption papers?

"All I'm saying," Sean said, turning the vehicle around to head in the direction of where Minnie was caring for Dylan, "is that you're a single woman."

"I know that I'm a single woman." So many comments came to mind, but part of the process in becoming a foster parent was learning better communication skills. She couldn't claim that fighting fair came easy, especially with Sean, but the class had taught her that disagreements were useful if genuinely trying to understand the other person. She took a deep breath. "I'm a little confused what you mean by that statement. I would think having a big dog would be an advantage, not a weakness, given that I'm single."

"You're alone. If something happened to you, what would become of the dog? Or what if the killer decides to come after the dog? What if he's angry you have it and decides to hurt either of you? What if the dog is hurt or, worse, dies? How would you *ever recover*?"

His last two words reverberated with emotion. She pressed her lips together. Where had that come from? The rapid list of scenarios and the way he gripped the wheel until his knuckles turned white set off alarm bells. Was *Sean* scared about something?

Her mouth went dry. Her gut insisted this wasn't about the dog.

He blinked rapidly and shrugged. "Just some things to think about tonight, I guess."

"I guess so," she replied softly, her mind still reeling. "Thank you for telling me what was on your mind, but I think I need to tell you what's on mine. Would you be willing to pull over for a second?" She'd like to avoid arriving to pick up Dylan as an emotional wreck.

He gave her a side-glance and frowned. "Of course. It's been a big day." He pulled over to the side of the road.

Grace made a sound in the back that sounded like half a whine and half a question. "Still off duty," Sean said softly. He twisted his torso to face her.

"Would you have the same opinion, the same questions for me to consider, if I told you I was applying to adopt Dylan?"

His form remained statuesque, but his pupils widened, darkening his eyes. He blew out a breath and his torso sagged in front of her. "I think we both know I saw the adoption papers back at your apartment."

"If it bothered you, why didn't you say something earlier?"

"Instead of resting it all on the husky, you mean?" He shook his head and offered a small smile. "You could always see right through me."

"Funny because I always felt like you were a mystery most of the time."

"I have no right to tell you what to do, Ivy. We both know that. But I've said it before. I still care about you, so I have these knee-jerk reactions. I'm trying to work through it." He scratched the top of his head. "I think I finally need to tell you something."

She held her breath. The promise of a secret terrified her. Would she finally find out why he'd changed so drastically early in their marriage?

He folded his hands and rested them on the bottom half of the wheel. "On my first call out with Grace—an earthquake discovery—I was convinced we would find people alive."

"Oh." The word came out as a hushed breath. "I didn't think she was trained to find—"

"Grace is not a search-and-rescue dog, if that's what you mean. But if she comes across a person who is still alive while she's working, she's going to react in some way. And I'd notice." He offered a sheepish grin. "Newbie optimism, I guess. Anyway, we were called out within seconds of the earthquake and only five minutes away."

"I remember that day. The chandelier swung in our dining room for like five minutes. You called to check on me before you went out on the call."

He nodded. "I'd hoped that we'd arrive fast enough to the scene. Grace alerted almost right away. Rescuers swarmed the area. We dug and moved the rubble as fast as possible and found—" His voice broke and he cleared his throat. "We found a woman... She looked remarkably similar to you." He spoke in a low, gravelly monotone. "And she had her arms wrapped around a child. The woman had already passed away, but the child stirred—at least, I thought she might have." He coughed. "But I was told the child was also already gone, too. We weren't able to save either one."

It was as if a grainy home movie rewound in her mind and replayed. Ivy questioned every interaction they'd ever had after that moment. She'd always assumed he'd never found anyone in that earthquake. He'd said Grace did great on her first run. That was all. Was that when he started dragging his feet into their home each day, drained? She couldn't be sure when that had started. Had she misunderstood him most of their marriage? "Your first call out," she said weakly.

"I didn't tell you to upset you. In my specialty, officers aren't encouraged to talk a lot about what we discover, especially with our families. Besides, it's best if we don't dwell too long. I didn't want you to hate my job. I had to work through it and figure out how to cope. Just because it was hard didn't mean I wanted to quit."

She nodded, because she wasn't sure what to say. Surely, he could've at least told her that he was having a hard time coping. *Couldn't* he have?

"I've learned it's best to focus on the good things and move on, but that discovery was my first and the hardest. I'm only telling you now because if you'd experienced what I have, then maybe you'd agree."

"Agree about what?" she asked softly.

"That there's so much pain and sorrow out there." He waved his arms, gesturing to the world outside the window. "You have to know, Ivy, that you'll face that kind of sorrow if you agree to adopt. If it's not a murderer threatening you, then maybe it's the choices Dylan makes later on. It's not a matter of if but *when*. And I'm not sure you've ever understood that agreeing to parent is assenting to a broken heart, on purpose. Do you really want that for yourself? To end up broken?"

She'd heard his argument against having children so many times that she had it memorized, but this was new. Entirely different. This time she finally comprehended the moment that convinced him that he shouldn't become a parent. No wonder he'd changed his mind all of a sudden. Her eyes burned with unshed tears, but she refused to cry for him, for them, for that mother and the child he'd found. Even though she desperately wanted to be alone and do just that.

Instead, she focused on the crumbling

building in front of them and took shallow breaths. The building was missing pieces of siding. Just like she'd been missing pieces in understanding Sean. It'd weakened them and led to their entire marriage crashing down around them. Her voice shook as she said the words that played in her head on a loop. "I guess I'm just in shock you didn't tell me about your first call out. That's a pretty big thing."

"To be fair, you never really asked me about that part of the job."

"I always asked about your day!" Her volume rose despite trying to stay calm. "I wanted to respect your professional boundaries if you couldn't tell me some things. What was I supposed to say? *Find any bodies today?*" She recoiled at her own words.

"Of course not." He shook his head. "I wasn't trying to start a fight. I was only trying to get you to realize how big a deal—"

"—having a child is. Yes, I heard you." All his other reasons he'd tried to convince her with over the years were overshadowed by this one. "I'm also hearing how much fear and control had a say in our marriage." She hung her head. "More than I'd thought. I'm sorry if that sounds harsh."

"What? No, I think you've misunderstood me. Ivy…" Radio static burst through the speakers.

"Sean, we need you at headquarters," Gabriel said. "Bring Ivy."

He let out an exasperated sigh. "Guess we're out of time." Sean shifted the SUV into Drive.

She faced forward, realizing his statement had more than one meaning.

EIGHT

Sean vibrated with energy as he parked in front of the trooper post. The few officers assigned to this post had to cover an area the size of West Virginia. So it wasn't unusual that the post was empty enough for the K-9 troopers to take an office. They shared the space with the Alaska National Guard Armory. The entire bottom section of the building was made of garages for the various vehicles needed, given the constant changing terrain. He led Ivy and Grace up a set of metal stairs to enter the main offices.

Each step on the metal stairs set his teeth on edge. He needed to let go of the last words Ivy had said to him, especially since he wasn't afforded the option to discuss it further. He should've never told her about that earthquake in the first place. Delving into things from the past was like stepping into an unmarked minefield. But he thought she'd understand that he was trying to keep her from making a mistake. A dog and a kid would make her even more vulnerable.

That first call had been on his mind more than usual lately. They had a new rookie trooper getting ready to join their ranks, Ian McCaffrey, with his newly-trained cadaver dog. A German shepherd named Aurora. Sean would be assigned to help show him the ropes and let Ian shadow him from time to time. It'd forced Sean to reevaluate how he'd handled his first year before he could offer any advice.

The unpleasant conversation with Ivy had left a bad taste in his mouth. She couldn't be right about the control thing, though. *Could* she? He almost scoffed aloud. There were plenty of things in his life outside of his control, his job being a prime example. Not five minutes had gone by since they'd left the vet before a work call had interrupted their conversation. Control was only an illusion in life, something he'd fully admitted when he'd recently decided to believe in God.

He reached the top step and offered Ivy a forced smile as he opened the door for her. She'd misunderstood him, that was all. Understandable, considering how someone had tried to kill her only an hour before. If a quiet moment presented itself later that day, maybe he'd try again.

"Over here," Helena called, poking her head out into the hallway, the third door to the right.

Sean let the door close behind them as they hustled down the hallway. They stepped inside the office in time to hear the colonel speaking through the desktop monitor station on the countertop.

"We need you back in Anchorage." Lorenza glanced down at something off the video conferencing camera.

A muscle ticked in his jaw. He *knew* this would happen. Now more than ever, he couldn't leave Ivy. The gunman had specifically aimed his shots at her, not the rest of the team. Sean took a step forward and opened his mouth to speak.

But Gabriel placed a hand on his shoulder before he could utter a word. "You and Helena are staying here in Nome, on the case. I'm going back to help with the reindeer case."

"Sean, good to see you," the colonel said. "Yes, we don't want the lead on Terrence Kapowski to go cold. Katie's counting on us."

"Understood, ma'am." He blew out a breath, releasing all the pent-up energy from being prepared to argue.

"Lorenza has some news on Ivy's case," Helena said. "That's why we needed you both here."

"Yes." The colonel offered a friendly smile. "Good to see you, Ivy. Sorry that it's under these circumstances. Appreciated you helping us out with the survivalist case recently."

"Not sure I was much help, but thank you," Ivy said. "I'm always happy to offer what I know."

Lorenza's smile faded as she addressed her fellow team members. "Now to the news. We're sending the results on the victim your way. Check your fax machine. Tala was able to find a match on the blood DNA of the victim. Let me share the most recent photo we have in the system."

The screen switched to a zoomed-in version of a Washington driver's license photograph. "'Francine McMillan,'" Sean read aloud.

Ivy blanched. "That's her. A few years younger and with different hair, but definitely her."

The fax machine roared to life. Gabriel gathered the papers that spit out. "Arrested on shoplifting a few years back. Last known address was near San Francisco. Nothing else of note that I can see." He passed the stack of papers to Helena to review, as well.

"So, our victim wasn't a resident, and we have no idea why she was in Alaska," Sean said.

"No idea what motive our suspect could have yet, either," Gabriel told Lorenza.

"Could've just been the wrong place at the wrong time," Helena mused. She frowned, reading over the papers. "Not getting any clues from her record, either."

"Maybe she lifted something off our suspect," Sean said.

"That would explain why he kept asking me where she'd put it," Ivy added. "You think this is a theft and a violent retaliation?"

Lorenza's eyebrows shot up at Ivy's interjection. "I'll leave it to you guys to take it from here. Sean, make it your priority to find the deceased. Helena, take the lead. Gabriel, have a safe flight. Check in tomorrow morning with me."

Gabriel agreed and signed off the communication.

The muscles in Sean's back wouldn't relax. While he was glad that Lorenza wasn't ordering him back home, the message had been clear. She wanted him to find the body and leave Ivy's protection to others. And he knew the moment they found the victim, Lorenza wouldn't hesitate to bring him back to Anchorage, whether or not they'd found the murderer. Professional courtesy, given his relationship to Ivy, only went so far.

"Can you make a copy of the license for me to take?" Ivy asked, jarring Sean out of his thoughts.

Helena frowned. "What'd you have in mind?"

"I'd like to ask Minnie if she recognizes the victim. Fiona may have her pulse on all the visitors who stay at her B and B, but Minnie knows all the locals and several from the nearby villages. She's lived here for ages."

"It's a good idea," Sean acknowledged. But they couldn't just hand Ivy copies of the reports. "I can show Minnie."

Gabriel moved to a desk monitor and took a screenshot of the license, cropping the photo so it only showed Francine's face, and printed it. He handed the printed photo to Sean and shook his hand. "Hope I'll see you soon back at base. But not too soon."

At least his teammates understood the importance of finishing this case. He gestured to the door with the photo. "Shall we?"

Gabriel flashed her a grin as she turned to leave with Sean. "And don't worry," he said. "These guys don't need *me* to solve the case."

"I wasn't worried until you said that," Ivy said, a teasing lilt to her voice. It didn't disguise the strain in her eyes and forehead.

Helena handed them each a hoagie from the sub shop across the street. "You need to keep your strength up. And say the word if you need to take a rest, Ivy. You still are recovering from a nasty bump on the head."

Sean studied the loose bun she had at the nape of her neck. He should've noticed it wasn't her usual style. Her head likely hurt too much to pull it back into her standard tight ponytail.

"Oh, and before I forget, there are a few empty rooms with cots and blankets down the hall, reserved for traveling troopers. They're available to us. This won't be luxury accommodations, but it'll be safe."

He nodded. "Agreed."

"I'm staying at the bunker," Ivy said.

"We can't force you, of course," Helena cut in before Sean could object. "But we do highly recommend you allow one or both of us to stay in the same location for your safety. At least until we have the shooter behind bars. This office is well protected."

"Yes, and as you mentioned, it's barebones. No offense to anyone, but it's not well suited for a toddler's needs. The bunker is already childproofed. There's plenty of room for you and Sean, if you're willing."

Helena raised an eyebrow but said nothing as she exchanged a glance with him. Judging by her expression, she was just as apprehensive as he was about the bunker scenario. He'd had enough dealing with survivalists lately; he didn't want to live like one, too.

"Give us until the end of the day before you decide, please," Sean said. "Maybe neither will be necessary."

"Okay. I think I'll take my sandwich to go. I'd really like to be with Dylan now."

"Of course." He was just as anxious to leave, but not for the same reason. Though, the thought of seeing Dylan again eased some of the tension in his muscles. Didn't mean he was changing his stance on having kids. He could find them amusing without wanting one of his own. It was human nature to enjoy a baby's laugh. It was in a dog's nature as well, if Grace was any indication.

Neither of them ended up eating their sandwiches, though, despite nearing late afternoon. Sean, for his part, knew the bread would taste like cardboard until the day was done. Now that the danger of the morning had fully passed, his brain replayed the shooting on a loop. He'd almost lost Grace and

Ivy in one go. But it hadn't happened. Maybe his prayers were being heard. Though, why God couldn't have also stopped the man from kidnapping Ivy and murdering Francine was something he might never understand. *That's why they call it faith.* Eli Partridge, their tech guru, had answered that to quite a few of Sean's questions.

He pulled up to the house they'd escorted Minnie to that morning. An unmarked police car sat on the corner with an officer who waved at them. "See? He was safe the entire time."

She strode ahead of him to the porch and knocked. Minnie answered with Dylan in her arms. "Doggy. Mama," the boy said, rubbing his eyes.

"I see where I am in the order of things," she said with a laugh and leaned over to kiss his cheek.

"Just woke up from his nap," Minnie said.

Sean turned around slowly, examining the houses and street around them. He was searching for any movement, any sign they'd been followed. "Do you mind if we come in and ask you a few questions?"

Minnie arched an eyebrow. "Am I a suspect now?"

Ivy laughed, pulling Dylan into her arms

and snuggling her cheek against his. "No. We just need to know if you recognize someone."

The babysitter led them into a kitchen decked out in cow-themed decor. A canvas at the far edge of the room featured a smiling cow whose eyes appeared to follow him with every move. "Dylan loves this house," Minnie said. "My friend Charla said we can use it all week if we need to." She reached out and squeezed Ivy's wrist. "For your sake, honey, I hope that's not true."

Sean held up the printout of Francine's photo. "Do you recognize her?"

"Oh, yes." Minnie squinted and stared at the ceiling. "Her name's on the tip of my tongue. She came to town a while back, can't say for sure how long, though. At least a few months. Saw her at one of the town meetings. She was asking around for seasonal work. Struck me as a snooty city girl at first, to be honest, but she said she had dredge experience. Was willing to do the cleaning and work her way up." The older woman shook her head and whistled. "Hard work, that job, and the least glamorous to volunteer for. You can't help but end the day soaked to the bone and covered in mud when you're first learning the ropes. And even then, it doesn't get much better." Minnie walked across the kitchen, opened the top of a cookie jar and waved at it. "Want one?"

Ivy shook her head. "Is that all you remember?"

Minnie's exhalation carried a hint of sadness. "I've seen loads of desperate hopefuls come around here searching for gold and find themselves exhausted, cold and dirty, with little to show for it. But she—oh, her name will come to me—she seemed ready to work. Demonstrated more knowledge than most who try to characterize themselves as experienced."

"Do you know if anyone hired her?"

Minnie finally selected a cookie from the jar and took a bite. "If she was still around, I imagine someone did. Most people know you, Ivy. They'll talk to you." She gave a side-eye to him as if to say, *Avoid bringing the stiff.*

Sean fought against rolling his eyes. He would do anything to keep Ivy safe, but the last thing he wanted to do was ask for her help in this case. *Again.* He held up the photo again. "Was she with a man?"

Ivy shot him a surprised look.

Minnie tapped her chin. "Maybe. Um…"

Ivy set Dylan back down next to the diaper bag of toys, but the boy reached for Grace. The K-9 sat down without Sean's command

and allowed Dylan to pat her head, a bit intensely. Sean took a knee to make sure the pats didn't turn to pulling out fur.

Minnie shrugged. "Having a hard time remembering anything about a guy."

Ivy blinked rapidly and straightened, lifting her hand above her head. "Was he about this tall and auburn hair—"

"Sorry, no. At least, I never saw her with anyone like that." An electronic buzzing filled the room. Minnie set down her half-eaten cookie and picked up the phone from the counter. "I don't recognize this number."

To Sean's surprise, she still answered it. "Hello?"

The woman had the volume of the phone on high, because the caller's deep voice rang through the room. "Good afternoon, ma'am. I'm an Alaskan State Trooper calling on behalf of Ivy West. She's running late, answering questions after today's incident. She would like you to bring Dylan and meet her—"

"Oh, is that right? She does, huh?" Minnie's outraged voice practically shook the walls. "That's funny since she's standing right in front of me! How *dare* you try—" She pulled her chin back. "He hung up!"

Sean scooped up Dylan, lest there be any

fur pulling while he wasn't looking, and crossed the room in two strides, taking the phone from Minnie. The sound of a disconnected line hit his ears.

The older woman crossed her arms across her chest. "Can you believe the nerve?"

Sean hit the button to look at the list of recent callers and took a heartbeat to memorize the number. He clicked the radio at his shoulder. "I need a trace."

Helena answered his call and took the number. A few moments later, she was back on the line. "Must've been a burner phone. Got nowhere."

He looked toward Ivy. Her skin had turned paler than a piece of chalk, and she grabbed a chair to steady herself. "He's after Dylan now," she whispered.

With all his precautions, his worst nightmares were coming to life before his eyes. Even though he hated it, deep down he knew it was time to go to the bunker.

Ivy rushed forward to hold Dylan. Sean's eyebrows rose, as if he'd forgotten he was holding him, even as the toddler repeatedly smacked the shiny name tag above Sean's uniform pocket. She wrapped her hands around Dylan's waist and pulled him to her.

He whined, which prompted Grace to mimic the whine. Dylan laughed so hard his forehead hit her chest hard. But physical pain was welcome compared to the chaotic thoughts running through her head.

"We need to know how he found out about Dylan, got Minnie's number..." he began.

"My phone. He used my phone." Her mouth went dry, imagining that man sifting slowly, methodically through every text, email and photo. "I wasn't sure it was real but had a vague memory of him using my thumb to touch something. He could've turned off the lock screen then and wouldn't need a cell signal to go through everything. Easy to take that information and use a different phone." She should've thought of that before. She'd let her hopes get up that Helena and the team would be able to track her phone down. "He already knew about Dylan because he saw him in the B and B. A quick read of my texts and anyone would be able to figure out Minnie was his sitter."

The store break-in was nothing compared to a murderer having access to what amounted to her digital diary. She imagined the auburn-haired man yanking Dylan from her arms. A chill went through her. Then her mind darted to the memory of the woman's fingers sticking out of the rolled-up rug, and she nearly keeled over.

Sean reached for her, his strong hands on either of her arms. "I think you need to sit down and eat that cookie Minnie offered, whether you want to or not. You haven't had anything since breakfast."

She'd eaten a huge breakfast, a rarity for her, so she didn't think that was the cause. The weariness in her bones kept her from arguing. She sat in the kitchen chair and allowed Dylan to go back to toddling around the room. He gave chase to Grace, who trotted just out of reach, then waited. Within seconds, the boy and the dog were in an epic game of keep-away.

She was watching something hilarious, something she'd love to remember someday. But her mind refused to cooperate and revel in Dylan's delight. She took shallow breaths as she nibbled on the cookie Sean had placed in her palm. A *cookie*! This was no time to be eating a treat when someone was intent on taking her son from her. Maybe he wasn't officially her son yet, but...

Her eyes burned and she placed her tongue firmly against the inside of her teeth to keep from crying. How would this affect the adoption? At the very least, she had to let the social worker know that the gunman was after Dylan. There was no time to allow herself to be scared or angry or even violated, despite being hit over the head with all three...

Sean clicked the radio, but his eyes didn't so much as flicker away from her face. "Any progress on pinging Ivy's phone?"

"Double-checking," Helena answered.

He crouched in front of Ivy and held her hand. "I know this is difficult, but we need to be careful not to make any knee-jerk reactions. We can't even assume it was the murderer on the phone."

"It *was* him." A cold sensation trickled from the top of her head and worked its way down, as if allowing her body to go numb.

Sean frowned and pulled her hands together, placing his other hand on top of hers, while two fingers slid to the inside of her right wrist. "Take deep breaths for me, Ivy, before we discuss this more. Your heart is working so hard right now you might be going into shock."

Shock would be welcome compared to the sensation before. Still, she needed her wits right now. Ivy knew she wouldn't be any use to Dylan if she succumbed to fear. So she pulled her hands from his and forced herself to eat the stupid cookie. Minnie rushed to the kettle and had a cup of tea in her hands three minutes later.

"You've got a little color again," she commented, nodding.

"Why'd you have to taunt him, Minnie?" Ivy's question slipped from her mouth without a filter. "We might've been able to keep him talking, trace him, set up a trap..."

The woman took a step back, hand to her reddening neck. "I wasn't trying to taunt him. I was furious he would even—"

Ivy set the tea down. Of *course* she didn't mean to. She dropped her forehead into her hands. "I know."

"I'm sorry. I didn't think of trying to keep him talking."

"Please forget I said anything. I didn't even think of it until now." All threads of civility had begun to unravel after the day's events. If she didn't get some time to herself soon, she feared what she might say next.

"I really am sorry, hon." Minnie reached for her shoulder and gave it a squeeze. "Don't lose hope. God is with you. Even now."

Ivy flattened her lips together and avoided eye contact as she nodded.

"You don't want to hear it now. Understood. I know it doesn't feel like it, but knowing He's with you is everything. Believing isn't a onetime thing. And you need that faith more now than ever, even when you can't see Him working."

Her eyes stung with hot unshed tears. Sean's phone rang and they both swiveled in his direction. He answered and mouthed Helena's name. "Okay," he said into the receiver. "No big surprise since so much of the area doesn't have a cell signal."

In other words, Helena wasn't finding any leads on her phone. Despite Minnie's encouragement, Ivy couldn't stay put anymore. Being kidnapped and shot at was one thing, but now the killer was after her son. She scooped up the diaper-bag strap and lifted it over her shoulder. "I need to go." She shifted Dylan to her left hip and walked out the door.

Grace ran in front of her path and stared, a challenge in her eyes.

"Seriously, Grace? He didn't tell you to protect."

"I think she's taken it upon herself to protect Dylan," Sean said softly. He nodded at Minnie. "Block that number. I don't want you answering again if he calls. And we need to discuss your safety. Maybe stay with your daughter tonight."

Ivy's gut grew hot. She hadn't thought of Minnie's safety.

"I think I'll do that," she said. "You two go on. I'll be fine."

"I'll let the officer know to stay here and follow you to your daughter's." Sean shook a thumbs-up sign at Grace. She ran around the back of Ivy's legs and moved to his side. They walked down the porch steps together.

Sean reached across her to open the door. "I know you're upset—rightfully so—but at least he doesn't know where we are."

"Let's keep it that way. Tell Helena if she wants to come with us, she needs to meet up with us at the hospital."

His eyes narrowed. "Your head injury? You *have* been looking really pale."

"I'm fine. The hospital is on the outskirts of town and the easiest place to meet up before heading to the bunker. I'm not giving directions over the phone. Not after what happened earlier."

"If you're worried about him following us, we are trained to spot—"

She held up a hand, fighting to keep a tight rein on her emotions. Like a frayed rope, the rein was barely intact. Before she could explain herself, Sean waved her to the SUV. "Helena says there are a couple of unmarked SUVs in the garage. How about we use those for extra protection. Then you don't need to worry that someone will recognize our trooper vehicles."

Nothing other than that creep being behind bars would help the worry go away, but she forced herself to nod. Ten minutes later, they hit the road in the two black SUVS. While better than having trooper logos on the side, two black vehicles still seemed suspicious in her mind.

They headed northeast toward Anvil Mountain, directly for the White Alice antennae, a now-abandoned and obsolete communications system the air force built during the Cold War in the '50s. There were apparently thirty other stations like it throughout Alaska, but Ivy was only familiar with this one.

The four antennae that made up White Alice stood massive in size, their own Stonehenge in appearance. The SUV bounced from side to side on the rough gravel road, lulling Dylan to sleep. Her own eyes grew heavy the farther they drove from town, but she was the one who needed to give directions. Just as they neared White Alice—which caused Sean to whistle low in appreciation—she pointed to what would easily be mistaken as an animal-trampled path to the left.

"That's not a road," he said.

"I'm aware, but it's flat and solid and you're already in four-wheel drive." In fact, no one could make it this far in a normal car, as the road wasn't maintained.

Sean made the sharp, bumpy turn and drove in between two hills. Only then could Ivy see the front of the bunker. The stairs led to the open tunnel near the top of the hill. The bunker had been built within the hill but had to be high enough to avoid getting buried in the snow during winter. Permafrost prevented anything from getting built underground. If a wayward backpacker came this far, they'd likely think the tunnel to be old and abandoned.

Dylan stirred in the car seat. Grace leaned forward and casually licked the top of his hand. "No. Doggy wet!" But judging by his smile, he was quite pleased the K-9 had licked him. If their caseworker said she could stay with him here on a more permanent basis, what would raising him in a bunker be like? This wasn't how she wanted to raise her own child, even though there was a lot she loved about survivalist living.

She'd been young, having just started middle school, when her parents hastily packed her and her siblings in an RV two days after a bombing in New York City. They'd traveled cross-country to the West Coast. From there, they took a boat to Alaska.

She stared back out the window at Anvil Mountain once again. At least she didn't have to run away to the other end of the country. But had she taken Dylan far enough away to keep them safe?

NINE

Sean cringed at the echo each step created. It was like walking inside a corrugated tin can that once had held baked beans. "Was this really the type of place you grew up in?"

Ivy shrugged. "The one we grew up in was built prefab. My parents had this one customized. I would say this one is a little better."

He tried to keep his jaw from dropping but couldn't. This was *nicer* than the one she'd been raised in? Ivy reached for the rust-covered door handle and pulled on it without using a key. "You don't lock the door before you leave?" They might have different definitions of what constituted as safe. He looked over his shoulder to see Helena mirror his apprehension. The hard cots at the trooper post were sounding better all the time.

The door creaked open and revealed another more modern white-covered steel door. Ivy flipped open a black lid above the doorknob, typed in a code, reciting it aloud for Sean and Helena's benefit, and pressed Enter. The sound of hydraulic locks opening preceded her shoving open the door with her foot. A gleaming white hallway with shoe cubbies, coat hooks and mats greeted them. Surprisingly modern.

Ivy kicked off her shoes underneath a bench and flipped on some switches for the air purifier, active electric, heat and water. She walked in farther to an open kitchen and living room complete with a rug, stainless-steel appliances and a wooden dining room table. Several wall hangings of various picturesque Alaska landscapes glowed with light, giving the appearance of looking outside through windows. Even though Sean knew the bunker was built into the hill, the fake windows offered him an odd sense of comfort. Like he wasn't actually at risk of being buried alive.

"This wasn't at all what I expected," Helena said, dropping her travel bag on a dining room chair and spinning around. "I feel like I've stepped inside a futuristic home. This isn't what comes to mind when I think of survival bunkers."

"The size of everything, including the toilet and laundry, is smaller and works a little different than what you're used to, but it's relatively comfortable," Ivy murmured. "My parents purchased a luxury model. This is on the lower end of that spectrum. I'd keep your coats on for a little while. The heat should catch up soon."

"What would be on the higher end of luxury bunkers?" Sean asked.

"Some millionaires have ones with aquaponics, fitness centers like rock walls, movie theaters, pools and…" She placed Dylan down on the rug and put a hand on her head. Her eyelids drooped. "Um…"

Sean rushed forward and placed his hand on her back. "I think it's time for you to take a rest." At least she wasn't as sickly white as she'd been back at Minnie's, but the exhaustion still strained her features.

Helena nodded. "Yes, the doctor said you should avoid too much excitement and concentrated focus. We've inundated you with both in one day."

"But I need to take care of Dylan and make dinner and…"

"We'll take care of both of those," he assured her. "I saw you struggle to stay awake during the drive. Take a short rest." When they were dating, they often took short day trips on his day off. Ivy had always been a night owl at heart, something that probably helped her in Alaska during the months when the sun never set. He'd taken it as a compliment when on their third day-trip date she'd fallen asleep while he was driving. He wasn't much of a conversationalist, so he wasn't offended, but he'd seen it as an indication she felt safe around him.

Ivy didn't look safe now. She glanced between both Sean and Helena. "Are you sure you can take care of Dylan?"

Helena sat in a squat next to Dylan and Grace. Luna had decided to take a snooze herself in the far corner of the room. "I've recently had experience with babies—well, *one* baby. My sister's. Go rest, Ivy. Between the two of us, we'll prep some dinner, and then we can reevaluate."

Sean looked into her eyes. "Please let us know if you need to go back to the hospital." Her shoulders sagged, and she nodded. There appeared to be four bedrooms. Three had queen beds and one had four bunk beds, so he suggested Ivy take the middle queen. That way Sean would stay closest to the front entrance and Helena would be closest to the emergency exit, which turned out to be a ladder leading to the top of the hill that the bunker was burrowed inside.

After seeing Ivy settled, Sean searched through the pantry. Helena found what appeared to be a trapdoor, labeled as Frozen Foods in the kitchen floor. They twisted the hydraulic lock open and lifted the heavily insulated panel to reveal a chest freezer, half buried. The permafrost nestled around the freezer in layers. Inside the chest, an assortment of frozen meats and vegetables were rock-hard.

Sean selected a package of ground beef and offered to cook dinner while his teammate took the first round of playing with Dylan. Mostly that involved making sure the eager toddler didn't get too rowdy with the dogs. It was amazing how much strength those little fingers could have when they locked down on something. As he browned the meat for dinner, he was reminded of all the little ones he'd interacted with over the last few months with the team.

His mind threatened to question every decision in the past, so he focused harder on the frozen beef. Amazing that the permafrost could work in a survivalist's favor here. Granted, most survivalists probably didn't have the luxury of such an upscale bunker.

The permafrost intrigued him. Even though there was grass and sage brush on the top layer outside, permafrost was frozen ground. Any type of frozen earth, whether soil or sediment or rock, all bound together as ice could make up permafrost. Near Anchorage, permafrost could be found, but only in isolated patches. In the Arctic, it was likely to be everywhere. Grace had worked in avalanches, but he couldn't recall a case with permafrost. She should still be able to detect through it. From what he could tell, the stuff looked rock-hard. How would that affect where the victim's body could be buried…?

"I'm feeling much better," Ivy said. She stepped into the kitchen, now dressed in light pink sweatpants and a sweatshirt that read Parenting Style: Survivalist.

"Nice sweatshirt."

She cringed. "I thought it was funnier before we actually headed over to the bunker. You were right, though. I just needed a few minutes to close my eyes. Smells delicious."

"Dinner's almost ready." He just about flinched. It sounded too natural to be in the kitchen together.

She didn't seem bothered. She picked up Dylan and nuzzled his nose. "Any new developments?" she asked in a singsong way as she grinned.

Sean stilled, wooden spoon in hand. It was

like seeing a distorted version of the dream life they'd spent hours imagining in those early months of marriage. He loved seeing her smile like that, in her element as a mother, loving on their boy. *Their* boy? He poured a can of crushed tomatoes in the skillet and stirred faster. Sauce splashed on his hand. He took a deep breath. He had no right to even think such a thing. Maybe he also needed a nap.

"Sean filled me in on what Minnie said when you showed her the victim's photograph," Helena said. "We'll go interview the dredge companies in operation tomorrow. Starting with the ones that parked in that lot."

Ivy nodded slowly. "That's good, but Minnie was right that I should go with you. People get touchy when you start asking too many questions about their gold operations. I know some of the employees already. Seasonal workers—usually new to the job and the area—can't afford to get a place to live, so they pick up gear at the mission until they make enough money to afford housing. The majority end up going back home." She sighed. "But I don't know if Minnie will be willing to watch Dylan again after what happened today." Her lighthearted tone turned somber. "Especially with how I reacted…"

"She will," Helena said. "I spoke to her on the phone while I was waiting for you to pick up the unmarked cars at the trooper post. And we have a uniformed officer willing to guard her friend's house again while she watches him."

Ivy shook her head. "She's a true friend. I don't deserve her."

"You didn't deserve to be kidnapped or targeted, either." Sean was struggling to keep his own thoughts positive, as well. The dredge operator interviews had potential, but the colonel made it clear his first priority was finding the victim's body. After their time near the shack, he was feeling hopeless on where to even start. But right *now*, he had a meal to put on the table. Sean used a fork to check the tenderness of the spaghetti noodles. "Dinner is ready."

Eating spaghetti with a thirteen-month-old proved a training exercise for Grace and Luna since the food was flung to all four corners of the bunker. The K-9 partners weren't allowed to eat on duty and were only allowed to enjoy their special food. Helena finished first and took care of their meals and a quick walk outside while Sean cleaned the kitchen. Ivy wiped up the considerable mess on Dylan and the walls. He began to fuss and whine.

"Did he even eat anything?"

She put her hands on her hips and studied him for a second. "If only food by osmosis worked." She laughed and their eyes connected. The warmth in his gut sobered him immediately. He turned back to find something else to clean. Except Dylan's fussing turned into full-on crying. Ivy offered him his favorite foods from the diaper bag and there was no interest. The dogs came back inside, but not even their appearance stopped his crying.

"I'm sorry," Ivy said over the noise, pacing with him in her arms. "Sometimes he does this. It's usually when he's overtired. And everything has been different the past two days. No routine. I don't think he had his full nap time today."

Grace moved to Sean's pack and placed her nose on the side pocket. His partner always surprised him with her intuition. "Good idea, girl." He hadn't intended to train Grace to perform whenever a child was unhappy, but after the past few months, they had performed for quite a few unhappy little ones while working cases.

"Uh-oh, I think this is my cue to get my earplugs and go to bed," Helena said. She grabbed her pack. "No offense, Sean. Come on, Luna. I'm not sure you'll appreciate this, either."

"Everyone's a critic," Sean said, causing Ivy to raise her eyebrows. "Grace and I have been alone a lot—often somewhere remote—and we sort of picked up a new hobby." He pulled out the harmonica.

Ivy's mouth dropped. "You learned to play?"

"That's *debatable*," Helena called out with a chuckle. She disappeared into her room and closed the door.

"You're not my target audience," Sean told Helena. He glanced down at Grace. "Ready? Here goes nothing." He took a deep breath and began to play the only song he really knew. The notes to "Twinkle, Twinkle, Little Star" amplified in the bunker as Grace howled along. She lifted her nose to the sky and managed to look as if she were crooning the notes. Dylan silenced midcry, staring at them both, wet cheeks and all. His little lip quivered, and then the smallest of smiles appeared.

Sean took a step back and stood with his legs apart, Grace's cue for the next part of the routine. The dog darted in between his legs and around in a figure eight while singing. Then it was Grace's turn to stand still while Sean marched around her. He tried to focus on only Dylan, but couldn't help but enjoy the way Ivy leaned back and watched him. By the time they reached the long final note, the toddler was giggling and clapping.

"Shall I play the 'ABCs' now?" Sean asked. "Or how about 'Baa Baa Black Sheep'?"

Ivy tilted her head, her eyes glistening. For a small second, he felt like her hero again and not the one who had caused her pain. "Don't those all have the same melody?" she asked.

He raised his hands. "Busted. We only know one song. Grace does the singing and dancing, and I provide backup."

Dylan yawned and rubbed his eyes. In a swift motion, Ivy offered him a blanket and slipped away to put him to sleep for the night. She returned in five minutes, beaming. "That was better than any bedtime story I could've told him. Thank you, Sean."

"You're welcome." He sat on the couch, reorganizing and repacking the contents of his pack. Even though the mood was much lighter between them now, he still hated how they'd left their last conversation about Dylan.

Sean blew out a breath. He needed to ask her a question but didn't want to cause any more emotional upheaval in one day. Still, it *had* to be asked before they called it a night. "I need to know everyone who knows this location."

"My parents, the social worker, and now you and Helena."

His eyebrows rose. "And that's all? You haven't talked about it with anyone else?"

Ivy leaned back into the couch cushion and reached up to dim the light coming from the faux window above her. "They're the only ones that know the actual location and have been here. I mean, Minnie knows *of* the bunker." Her eyes widened. "And I guess my friend Marcella knows."

"Marcella?" It took him a moment to remember Ivy's friend. "The one that still lives in Fairbanks?" He knew it'd been hard on Ivy to live so far from her good friend.

"You remembered. She actually owns the mission. When she heard we'd…" Ivy hesitated. "…*divorced*," she continued, in a softer tone, "well, she knew I was planning to live in the bunker. She offered me the job. She visits in the summer and during the Iditarod, and I'm happy to share the apartment during those times."

Sean walked to the front door and checked the security panel. It was reassuring that her parents had made safety a priority. In addition to the armed security system, there was a perimeter alarm engaged and a gun case. He hesitated. "You really haven't talked about this place to anyone else?" He turned to face her. "Just in passing, even? A date, maybe?"

Her eyes widened and she quickly looked down at her clasped hands. "No."

"Is there anyone in Nome that might be wondering why you've dropped off the grid?"

Her lips curled up. "Are you still asking me because of the case, or is this conversation of a more *personal* nature?"

"What if it's a little of both?"

"I haven't been seeing anyone. Is…uh… anyone waiting for you to get back to Anchorage?"

He hated that her asking pleased him so much. "No."

An awkward silence hung in the air before she smiled. "I think I better get as much rest as I can before Dylan wakes up."

"Okay. Only one more question. Does the social worker know you're here right now?"

She pulled her knees up to her chest on the couch and wrapped her arms around them. "I used the burner phone Helena gave me and called her at the trooper post while you were installing Dylan's car seat in the SUV. She said as long as you were offering us protection, there shouldn't be a problem, but—" her voice cracked "—I'm still only a foster mom, so I can't really make a decision to run away with him. Even if it is for his own safety. I'm a realist. I know if that man isn't caught soon, you'll get called back—"

The pain in her voice was like a vise grip on his heart. "Ivy, I promise you I'm not leaving until that man is behind bars."

"*Don't*. I'm not holding you to that." She stood and offered him a sad smile. "We've been down the road of promises we couldn't keep. Let's not do that to ourselves again. Good night, Sean."

His breath caught, taken off guard that a simple good-night punched him in the gut with the same intensity as the moment he'd signed the divorce papers.

Ivy slid out from under the quilt with regret. The bunker never got hot, despite the heater running. She blamed the permafrost just underneath the flooring, which also was heated. Dylan's outstretched arms warmed her, though. She hesitated at the threshold. She needed Sean, yet she bristled anytime he came to her rescue. Once he got the guy, he'd be leaving. If she let her guard down, it would be harder to patch her heart up for the second time.

Shoulders back and head on straight, she stepped into the kitchen to find Helena hard at work, making waffles. The smell of maple, sugar and coffee brewing could almost fool her into believing everyone was gathered for fun. They worked around each other as Ivy prepped Dylan's oatmeal. Sean joined them just as they sat down at the table, though Ivy found it hard to sit so close to him. It was too much of a reminder of all the times they'd shared breakfast together in years past.

She felt Helena's stare before finally looking up. The trooper was alternating her stare between Ivy and Sean. "Did I miss anything last night?" she asked.

"Nope," Sean said, a little too quickly to sound normal. Ivy shrugged, unsure of what to say.

Helena raised her left eyebrow. "Okay, then. I'm curious about this survivalist lifestyle. Did you really grow up like this?"

She got the question often in her line of work. And there was no textbook answer for what she found they really wanted to know. "There are different types of survivalists. The type often depends on the motivation that inspired the change of lifestyle. For instance, my dad was a hedge fund manager who missed country life and my mom was an anthropology professor who wanted to be a homesteader. We lived in New York, and when there was a bombing, they suddenly believed moving out here would be the only way we'd survive. They cashed out their retirement savings and we made our way to Alaska. When things calmed down, they decided they liked living in the middle of nowhere. After my sisters and brother left for college, they decided to go back to the lower forty-eight and build up their retirement again." Ivy gestured at their surroundings. "They vacation here every summer, though."

"Did all your siblings stay in Alaska?"

"Spread out, but yes. Aside from the mosquito swarms, we love it here. Other survivalists are motivated by staying off the grid, distrustful of government. Some just have a love of living off the land, and then you have those who are running away from something. Like that missing-bride case you mentioned."

For the first time, it struck her that her parents really fell into the category of running away from something. They'd always focused on how they wanted to try living off the land anyway, but the reason they had was because they were fleeing from potential danger. Wasn't that her first instinct whenever trouble came her way, too?

She'd been a hypocrite. The thought smacked her fully awake. She'd been angry with Sean for letting fear have the deciding vote in their marriage, yet she let fear rule her heart plenty of times. She didn't want to disregard wisdom, though. Getting enough distance from the issues to figure out which was which proved almost impossible. She lifted up a silent prayer. *I need Your help.*

Helena pulled her hair back into a ponytail. "Sean mentioned you were a survivalist instructor but didn't want to raise Dylan the same way. Is hiding here hard for you?"

His neck turned red, a sure indication that he was worried Ivy wouldn't be pleased he'd shared that tidbit. "Well, Sean isn't wrong, but I wouldn't mind bringing Dylan here under different circumstances. I suppose that may seem contradictory, given my line of work. I still think they're useful skills, but the isolation and some of the hardships I experienced seemed unnecessary. A lot of benefits came from it, too."

Ivy gestured at the glowing images of the tundra on the walls. "You have to appreciate your surroundings wherever you are in order to stay alive. A certain amount of flexibility is required. Thinking outside of the box. And I love the quiet of nature."

She sighed, remembering the constant hum of traffic in Anchorage that set her teeth on edge. "In college, I discovered I enjoyed teaching those skills to others. There's something about being in nature. It's much easier to believe that God's in control and I'm not when I'm out there. And a little overwhelming to realize that such beauty was all created for more than our survival but also our pleasure." Ivy cradled her coffee mug. She'd gotten carried away and probably had said too much. "Anyway, I worked for the college fitness center, taking students on weekend adventure trips in the area. I loved it so much I took a job as a survival instructor after graduation."

"And that's how I met you." Sean beamed at her as if he were proud. The expression caught her off guard. "I knew I'd be in all sorts of remote areas as a trooper and wanted to be sure I had what it takes."

The memories of that week hit her in the gut. She had to tone down the emotions and keep the conversation professional. "That's right. You were an excellent student. Ever had to do a waterfall jump as a trooper?"

His eyes twinkled as he leaned forward on his elbows. "Can't say that I have."

Heat filled her cheeks. She shouldn't have alluded to that afternoon. Shortly after that practice jump, he'd kissed her behind the waterfall. *What* a first kiss!

Ivy stood and moved to attend Dylan, except he was perfectly content for once. She stood there, unsure of how to busy herself, her cheeks on fire.

Helena also left the table. "Come on, Grace. Do your morning walk with us."

Sean straightened. "Oh, you don't have—"

Grace and Luna flanked her on both sides. "We'll be able to pack up and leave faster. You can help Ivy clean up."

Ivy didn't miss the sly smile on Helena's lips as she stepped out of the bunker with the dogs. If Sean's teammate was trying to play *re*-matchmaker, she was barking up the wrong tree.

"Do you remember when you called to ask me for forgiveness, back in March?"

Sean's question only increased her discomfort. She nodded. Dwelling on the humbling moment wasn't the most pleasant, but her reasons had been. "I needed to let go of some unresolved stuff keeping my heart hard. Owning up to my part of the divorce helped." She wondered now, though, if her heart was really resolved.

"Really surprised me. You didn't ask me to apologize for my part, even though…" He cleared his throat. "Well, we both know I could've handled things better, too." Dylan began to fuss. Ivy turned to pick him up, but Sean scooped him up first, much to the boy's delight. She blinked rapidly, warring emotions building in her chest. What was he *doing*? Where was this headed?

"I went to work the next day and told Eli about your call." Sean made a funny face at Dylan, who tried to mimic him by scrunching up his nose. "I hadn't noticed the cross on Eli's desk before—at least, not consciously. He helped me understand. I've been wanting to tell you, but I don't know what's been holding me back."

"Are you trying to tell me you're a believer now?"

"Back in April." Sean turned to face her, and Dylan followed his gaze. "I guess I can't help but wonder if we had both…"

The two most important guys in her life watching her, together, took her breath away. She knew what Sean meant. If they'd both had faith, would they have handled things differently? "I've asked myself that, as well."

Sean set the boy down with a couple of toys from the diaper bag. "And about yesterday. I think you misunderstood me if you thought it was about control—"

"Sean, I'm not sure I'm ready for this conversation." Like a switch being flipped, her entire body tensed. He wouldn't dare try to convince her not to adopt again, would he? "I'm going to need a little more time to process what you told me. Don't get me wrong. I'm glad you told me about your first recovery and how it affected you. I always wondered why the sudden change—"

"It wasn't sudden." He stood and crossed his arms over his chest. "All the reasons I listed had always been issues."

"Yes, ones we'd discussed before we married, and yet agreed, *together*, that they weren't enough to deter us from starting a family. So, when you went back to those same bullet points a year into our marriage, I thought you were trying to hide that the real reason you didn't want kids was because of me."

He pulled his chin back. "What? What do you mean?"

"You thought I'd be a bad mother since I couldn't even handle city living." The words slipped out, words she'd been determined never to voice aloud.

"No. Why would you think that?" He moved forward, closer to her.

She automatically took a step back, her legs pressing against the edge of the table. "You are amazing with children." She waved at Dylan. "You clearly love kids, and they love you. So, I thought it had to be me. I was never a needy mess in small towns, but all my strengths seemed useless in a city." She whispered, "And you were never there."

"Ivy, I'm sorry I ever made you feel that way." He straightened and ran a hand through his hair. "I admit I got frustrated, but it was at myself. I knew I was failing you. We never went backpacking and adventuring like I said we would. That first year of working recoveries, I… I didn't handle the transition well. I think I was depressed but wasn't ready to acknowledge it, even though it'd been my dream to be part of the K-9 Unit." He pulled in a breath. "But it was never about not wanting to have a child with *you*."

They stared at each other, and Ivy couldn't look away, despite how blurry her vision had become. Her perspective shifted once more, coloring the memories different shades than they had been before. "All our arguments seem to have different meanings now." Her breath shuddered.

He reached for her and wrapped his arms around her. "I'm starting to feel the same." His voice, low and soft, made her stomach flip.

She closed her eyes, willing the burning

sensation to go away. She wouldn't cry. Instead, she rested her cheek on his chest. The uncomfortable stiffness in her muscles and bones suddenly evaporated, her entire body relaxing into his strength. Oh, how she'd missed being wrapped up in his strong embrace. This was how it was at their happiest. To be with him, to be married. He was always eager to touch her, comfort her. In his arms, everything was okay.

And she knew she could face anything as long as they were together.

But they *weren't*. She stepped back and offered him a small smile. They could've handled things so much differently, but it was too late. He still didn't want a family, despite the impression he loved being with Dylan. "And yet…some things haven't changed at all."

His mouth dropped open, but he seemed at a loss for words.

"I'm glad we both have changed for the better," she whispered. "We can be happy for each other." The front bunker door slammed. She couldn't bear to continue this conversation in front of Helena. She moved to the pack she'd brought from the survivalist mission. There had to be some tissues handy there.

She clumsily opened the bag and it tipped over. A canister resembling a giant tin of coffee fell out of the sack, and the lid popped off and rolled across the room. Packets of powdered water purification packets tumbled out, along with a glass jar that rolled to the tip of Ivy's feet. A glass jar shouldn't have been in there. She stretched to pick it up but froze before her fingers reached the glass. The light caught the contents and reflected yellow hues around the room. "Sean, I think I know what the man is searching for."

TEN

Gold. Everything about this case pointed to gold. He felt more like a sheriff in an old Western than a trooper trying to solve a murder case. The jar contained the purest flakes he'd ever seen, as well as pebble nuggets. Gold had reached almost two thousand dollars an ounce, so that hefty jar had to be worth a pretty penny. Helena had the jar right now, though, processing it for evidence and checking the glass and lid for fingerprints.

"So Francine must have wanted to escape with the gold. Why else would she have come to the mission?" Ivy tapped her knee with her finger as they drove through the streets of Nome, having already settled Dylan and Minnie back at a safe location. "Except the mission is practically made of windows. So maybe she came inside to get gear, but saw the man coming, so she stuffed the jar in one of the closest containers, thinking she could come back for it after she got rid of the guy."

"Your theory means she had to know her murderer," he said.

"She must have, otherwise why hide it?"

"Maybe he saw her with the jar of gold somewhere else and had been stalking her from her previous location. We can't rule out any possibilities without more evidence."

He pulled into the parking lot, noting the dredge the man had shot at them from. No sign of movement. "Let's start with the dredge that Minnie's son and daughter own."

Ivy pointed to the eighty-foot-long one. "It's the biggest one. They have the most employees, so that's a good choice."

"It's gigantic."

"They use it in the Norton Sound. Minnie said they spent over a million dollars to get it fixed up recently."

Sean whistled. "They find that much gold each year to make that a safe investment?"

"I can only assume so," she replied. "Minnie says they're like third-or fourth-generation miners, so they know what they're doing."

He parked in a way that would ensure he'd be the first to take any hit if someone was hiding on any of the other dredges. He escorted Ivy and Grace around the backside of the first dredge. Two men stepped out onto the top deck of the boat, twenty feet above them. Sean placed an arm out and Grace uttered a warning growl. "I know them," Ivy said, reaching her arm up and waving. "It's Ben, Fiona's husband, from the inn. And his son, Nathan."

"Hi, Ivy. Minnie said you'd be stopping by."

They climbed up the ramp that was still on the back end of the boat. The smells of fish and bleach warred with each other. Grace opened her mouth and scrunched up her nose, her teeth bared. "I know, girl," he said softly. She didn't like the smell of bleach, but it also wouldn't stop her from smelling the scent of death. "Get to work."

They maneuvered in between the equipment that seemed to fill every nook and cranny. So far, other than her huffs, Grace didn't alert on anything. The aluminum stairs led them to the top deck and, thankfully, to fresh air.

The lines in the older gentleman's face indicated the man had either been smiling or squinting most of his life. He offered a beefy hand to Sean. "So your Ivy's..." He let go and let the unsaid words hang.

"My ex," Ivy finished for him. "And he's kept me safe this past week."

"I know Minnie said we might be able to help you, but I don't really see how. She said you're in some kind of trouble, but she wouldn't tell us much more."

Sean pulled out the photograph of the victim, Francine. "Actually, we only need help in identifying this woman. Have you seen her before?"

The two men exchanged a meaningful glance after scanning the picture but didn't say anything.

"You know her, then," Ivy pressed. "It really would be a help if you told me about her."

Nathan scratched his head. "She was a big mistake, that's what. She worked for us for a couple months. Came highly recommended and knew how to talk the talk."

"Until she walked away with almost a hundred thousand dollars' worth of gold," Ben muttered. "She swindle you, too, Ivy?"

Her jaw dropped. Sean reached over and gave her hand the smallest of squeezes to indicate she shouldn't answer. The touch, though, sent warmth shooting up his arm, and he let go of her fingers at once.

"To be fair, we don't know if she robbed

us," Nathan said. "Not for sure. It's not as if we saw her do it."

Ben rolled his eyes. "Olivia had our Nathan wrapped around her little finger."

Nathan's neck reddened. "Dad, she didn't. She was a decent employee, then one day disappeared."

"Olivia?" Sean asked. If Francine McMillan was her real name, the woman had used an alias here.

"Yeah. Olivia Truby."

"If you were worried, why didn't you report her missing?" Ivy asked.

"We did, but the local cops told us we'd been duped." Ben turned back to the hoses he'd been wrangling when they had boarded. "Apparently, her driver's license and Social Security number were fakes."

"You said she came recommended," Sean said.

"Yeah, by one of the top mining district companies." Nathan turned to his father. "I did my due diligence. Her references checked out."

Sean felt like they were hearing an argument that had been played many times before. "Can I get those phone numbers from you?"

Nathan's shoulders sagged. "Sure, but they won't do you any good. Used to be one of the top mining district companies until their claims dried up a few years back. That's why I thought she was looking for work elsewhere, but when I called them after she went missing, all the numbers had been disconnected."

Ben shook his head in disgust. "Come to find out the owner had died several months before we hired her. Who knows who Nathan actually was discussing Olivia's references with."

Maybe they were dealing with a con gone wrong, then. "Ever see another man with her? Maybe a fellow employee with auburn hair?"

Nathan's eyebrows shot up. "No. That her boyfriend or something?"

His dad seemed to have pegged him right. The man had been smitten, which made it easier to be fooled.

"We're not sure. But do you know who owns the claims, the district, now?" Ivy asked.

"No. We figured the cops were right and left it at that." Ben wagged his finger. "But you could always check the Alaska Mapper."

"Of course," Ivy said, nodding. Sean had heard the name before but couldn't remember what it was. They said their goodbyes and left, without Grace having alerted.

Once back in the SUV, he turned to Ivy. "Alaska Mapper?"

"All gold claims have a paper trail now. I believe they went digital when the Department of Natural Resources started auctioning mining leases again, roughly ten years ago. Ben works in the Norton Sound, but there are still lots of smaller claims around all the rivers and creeks throughout the tundra. You can buy, sell or inherit claims as long as the permit fees are kept up to date. If we can use your computer at the trooper post, I can show you in person."

Sean headed for the post as she'd suggested. He needed to do a quick run on the Olivia Truby alias, as well.

"At least we know Francine was up to no good, otherwise why the fake name? And why couldn't we tell them that we found their gold?"

"It's evidence and we don't know they're the owners for sure yet."

"No assumptions." She nodded. "Right."

Her words hit him funny. While it was his motto while he worked a case, he'd certainly failed to do the same in their marriage. But right now he had to focus on the matter at hand. "Since Ben reported the missing gold to the local police, it's likely they'll get it back when we're done with it."

"Does any of this help us get closer to getting the guy? Maybe we could use the jar of gold as bait and you can lure him out."

"Maybe." He pulled into the trooper post and they found Helena in the office, hanging up a phone.

"Just touched base with the team," she said. "No fingerprints on the jar of gold except for the murder victim. It was a fast match since we'd just identified her." Helena pointed at Sean. "I'm eager to hear how the interview went, but excuse us, Ivy. I need to update Sean on some things in private."

Ivy pointed to another desktop computer. "May I? I'd like to start looking at Alaska Mapper."

Sean reached over and clicked a guest account that would keep her from clicking on any classified information and followed Helena into the hallway. "Sensitive news?"

"Possibly." Helena pulled her lips back in an apologetic grimace. "The troopers that've been on location in Little Diomede have wrapped up. They're on their way back here late this afternoon. The colonel says she'll give us another twenty-four hours. Then she needs us back. The troopers at this post can take over for us."

A sour taste rose up in his mouth. Ivy's assurances that he shouldn't promise anything came to mind. "Thanks for telling me." He didn't know how Lorenza would respond to his request for leave. Ivy might not even agree to let him protect her without Helena's presence, as well. If he thought about it too much, he wouldn't be able to focus on using the time they had left. His teammate eyed him for a second as if she didn't believe he was taking the news well before they walked back into the office.

"I think I've found something," Ivy said. He and Helena hovered over her shoulder as she zoomed into an online map with a box labeling the area as Bozsan mining district. "Ben and Nathan should've checked the Mapper before they called those numbers. They would've seen beforehand that the ownership was recently transferred to a trustee." She turned around. "Maybe you guys can get somewhere with that?"

Helena grabbed a notepad and jotted down the information. Then Sean moved to the computer next to Ivy and did a search for the mining district itself. A mining journal website filled with personal ads for gold claims filled the screen. *Top-tier gold deposit. For sale. Twenty State of Alaska placer and lode claims encompassing nine hundred acres. Recently mined forty troy ounces in one week.*

Proof of gold to serious buyers. Start mining gold nuggets immediately. $2,000,000.00 for recent mine, claims, camp and equipment. Contact Marty Macquoid. Agent.

The ancient clacking keyboard Helena's fingers were tapping stilled. "That name isn't in our system. No Marty Macquoid. But—" she inhaled sharply "—the district used to own that building next to the dredge parking lot."

"The one that our suspect ran into?" Sean blew out a breath. "Ben and Nathan Duncan indicated this mining district had dried up."

"True," Ivy said. "But if I follow your advice not to assume anything, then I can tell you that just because a claim dried up a few years ago doesn't mean they can't find more gold. This district surrounds a few creeks. They can also do hard-rock exploration." She paused. "You can't dig up the whole land, though. They only own the mineral rights of gold, so there are restrictions. This also uses a different type of dredging than Ben and Nathan do in the sea. It's possible there's potential for more gold to be found, but it's suspicious."

He stepped closer to her and looked at the mining map still on the screen. "I can't really tell where these claims are. This is an unusual map."

Ivy squinted at the screen. "I think I can help you with that." She turned to the map of the area the troopers post had laid out on the table in the center of the office. "See this?" Her finger traveled from the sea up a river. "This is the Niukluk River. There are countless creeks stemming from it, though you never know when they'll be dry or flowing during this time of year. It depends on how hot the summer was. The claims start—" Her finger froze in the air and her face paled.

Sean stepped closer. "Is this as close to where you were kidnapped as I think?"

"It's on the other side of the river." She inhaled and nodded. "But yes. Fairly close."

"So, if he took the body on the boat—"

"Like we thought, the body would've likely been discovered on a bank nearby by now. With the low water levels in places, something would've snagged it."

"Let's explore the theory that this is about the gold claims," Sean said. "The ad indicates there would be proof of mined gold."

"Olivia—I mean, *Francine*—could've stolen the gold for him." Ivy's eyes widened. "Maybe she double-crossed him and decided to run off with the gold instead of letting him use it to swindle some buyers."

"You think he was planning to pass off the stolen gold as gold recently found, even though the claims are actually dry." Helena tapped her finger on her chin. "If our suspect thinks he can scam someone out of two million dollars, that's motive for murder and reason enough to stick around until a sale," she said. "Let's keep working this angle."

Sean paced the space in front of the door, with Grace by his side. He often had his best ideas while moving around. "What if the body was buried somewhere on the land he currently owns?"

"He doesn't own the land, though. Only the claims." Ivy shrugged. "But it's not like anyone is living on the land, so it would be deserted."

Hope rose and quickly crashed. "If he's strategic about where he buried the body, it's possible it could never be discovered."

"Perhaps. But if he doesn't know the area well enough, then the body will be discovered on its own during the summer."

"What?" Sean stopped pacing and tried to decipher what she'd just said. He remembered the way the food kept cold underneath the bunker. "Permafrost?"

"Exactly. You can only dig about two feet before hitting rock-hard permafrost. Even the cemetery in town has to use an excavator. If it's not buried deep enough when the warm months hit the top layer, some frost melts and the waterlogged soil lifts up…" She shrugged. "Well, let's just say they've learned how deep they need to dig to prevent unpleasant surprises."

Sean didn't want to imagine that scenario. "But the riverbank has trees, so the soil there must be softer."

"Except the river surges every spring." Ivy tapped the map. "Ice chunks float toward the sea but get caught up all the time. Flooding is inevitable. Unless the murderer was fine with risking the body appearing after winter—"

"Which he wouldn't be if there was a way to trace him after the sale of the gold claims," Helena said. "If he had shown up with the jar of gold and sold the claims, there'd be no way to prove he scammed the buyers out of their money. Gold dredges flop all the time. It's a known risk."

Ivy gasped. "I should've realized."

"What?"

"On the opposite side of the river is the abandoned townsite I told you about. Even though it's not recommended, a number of foolhardy tourists try to drive across. Nome keeps an excavator over there specifically to help pull stuck tourists out. The gold claim intersects close to where they keep the excavator."

"Is it possible the suspect is hiding out somewhere on the thousand acres?" Helena asked. "The ad mentioned a camp."

Sean joined Ivy at the map. "I need to get Grace there. Time to be foolhardy and try to get across that river, too."

Ivy glanced at him. "Good thing you used to be married to an expert."

Ivy reversed and maneuvered the SUV for a third time. Grace grumbled a warbly commentary. "I don't need back-seat drivers, Grace."

"Welcome to my world," Sean said, laughing.

"It's imperative to get the best entry and exit points of the river for a crossing. Put Helena on the radio and make sure she follows my exact wheel movements as she follows us." Ivy geared up right to the edge of the gravel and thought through her technique. She'd already disconnected the fan belts in both vehicles and checked the air intake to ensure water wouldn't flood the engines.

The river's water levels were constantly fluctuating as well as the currents, developing class one and two rapids at various times of the year. At the moment, the waterway seemed calm with ripples over the rocks. "I think the murderer knows the area well."

"Something new convince you?"

"All of this is happening after September fifteenth, when fishing is no longer allowed. You won't see locals from nearby villages rafting down here anymore." She accelerated and felt the give in the steering wheel as she moved slow and steady through the waters, watching the bow wave move from front to back. "Tell Helena to take a sharp turn left after the rock on the right." They swayed side to side with the movement, driving over rocks below the surface.

Sean parroted her instructions on the radio as she reached the other side of the river. "You want to tell her anything else?"

"Gas up slow and steady up the incline. Stop immediately once out of the water."

Ivy parked at a diagonal, ensuring Helena had space to get past the mud, and hopped out. Rivulets poured out from the wheelbases like mini waterfalls. Stopping so soon helped prevent erosion of the exit point. She reattached both the fan belts and made quick work to get them driving again. Once again, the day was moving faster than anticipated.

Her thoughts drifted to her little boy. Even with an unmarked patrol car keeping an eye on the house where Minnie watched Dylan, none of it settled her nerves. She fought to keep her focus on what was right in front of her because Sean would be leaving tomorrow. Except he didn't know that she knew. She'd always teased him that he didn't know how to properly whisper, and it seemed Helena shared the same affliction.

He was being ordered home.

She'd be alone. *Again.* And Dylan wouldn't have Sean to pick him up and smile at him and play his harmonica…

She swallowed against the tightness in her throat. With his departure, her chances of being able to keep Dylan while a crazed man was still after her would dwindle. Her nose began to burn. Helena said the other troopers would take over her case, but they wouldn't spend every waking minute making sure Ivy and Dylan were safe. The least she could do was adopt that husky. Then Dylan would have a dog and a live security system.

She pulled up to the side of the abandoned warehouse where the excavator was parked.

"Stay in the vehicle, please. I'll only be

a moment." Sean leaned forward as if to give her a quick peck goodbye and froze, inches from her lips. His eyes widened and he reached his hand out to tap the steering wheel. "Uh, I guess I don't need the keys. Be right back." He jumped out of the vehicle and released Grace to run by his side.

Ivy sat stunned. He had been about to kiss her. As if they were married again, like part of a daily routine to kiss his wife every time he said hi and goodbye. Ivy's pulse hammered against her chest. Her imagination could be exaggerating. She flicked the key ignition to roll down the driver's-side window for some air.

"Look at the control panel." Helena's voice carried. "I'd guess someone hot-wired this recently."

Grace trotted to the portion with the claw and bucket. The dog sat down and stared at Sean. "She alerted," Ivy whispered aloud.

Sean and Helena ran back to the vehicles, their dogs beside them. He stopped at the door. "I'd like to drive now. Grace has the scent and she pointed north."

"To the mining claims." Ivy ran around to the passenger door, and within seconds, Sean gunned the SUV down a gravel path, past several buildings. A glimpse of something red caught her peripheral vision, and she twisted to find an ATV with a helmeted driver sitting, watching them. "Sean...there!"

He glanced in his mirror and slammed on his brakes. The ATV revved and turned due north on a gravel road, kicking up mud as it vaulted up and over a hill. Sean hit the radio button. "It might just be a joyride coincidence, but it's too suspicious not to at least ask a few questions."

He flipped on his sirens, but the ATV made no signs of stopping. After half a mile, the path abruptly stopped. Sean hit his palm against the dash. "Is this really another dead end?"

Ivy strained to look out the window. "No. Tracks in the tundra due northwest." She hesitated a second to get her bearings and confirm they were where she thought. "He's heading directly to that set of mining claims."

Sean gunned the vehicle northwest. The radio squawked. "I'm calling for backup," Helena said. "Let's hope we have some off-road support available to join us."

Ivy tensed, gripping the handle on the ceiling of the SUV, as they bounced over a particularly rocky terrain. "Sean, there are so many creeks in the area the ground is unreliable. It can be rocky, then covered in brush, then suddenly go sof—"

"Got it."

She wasn't so sure he really understood the unique natures of tundra. While much drier than the spring, there were still marshes and bogs. Her teeth chattered at the speed he was navigating, following the ATV's path. They rounded a foothill and the ATV was in their sights.

"Can you tell if it's him?" Sean asked, his focus never veering from the windshield, a challenge considering the increasing mud splatters. She squinted at the retreating form but had no way of knowing how tall a man was when he was sitting and bouncing over rough terrain. The black helmet covered all signs of his hair color, and they were too far away to notice his shoes.

"No," she said. "I'm sorry." They drove parallel with a creek on their left and a creek on their right, roughly six hundred feet apart. Worrisome. She wondered if Sean noticed as well, but as long as he was careful to stay on firm ground and the two creeks didn't intersect anytime soon, they should be okay. The ATV driver twisted to see them and changed direction suddenly, veering up and over another hill and disappearing. Sean accelerated and mud spattered the side windows, obscuring their visibility.

"Sean, maybe we should wait for—" Gravity took hold, and they dropped several feet. A scream escaped her at the sudden plunge. Grace barked until the vehicle stilled.

Sean turned to her, white as a sheet. "What just happened?"

"I think the ground just gave way." She pressed her forehead against the window and found the mud had already risen up to the middle of her door. "We're stuck in a mud hole."

Sean glanced in the rearview mirror. "We've lost Helena!" He grabbed the radio. "Helena? Are you okay?"

"Yes. Popped a tire before you rounded that last bend."

"We've lost him, but we will need a tow truck."

Ivy shook her head. "You need the dozer. It's the only thing with enough power to pull us out, just like the tourists who get themselves in trouble. Ask for Max. He volunteers his time to do this." She dropped her forehead in her hands. As soon as the locals got word she needed saving like this, she would never live it down.

Sean gritted out the request. They sat in

awkward silence for a minute, though he was constantly twisting in his seat, presumably trying to come up with another solution.

"Dispatch said they had already called Max on standby when I asked for backup here," Helena relayed through the radio. "Guess it's common to get stuck."

"I should have known better," Ivy said with a groan. She'd worked so hard to get accepted as a true local instead of the transplant she'd first been considered. "ATVs are easier to get unstuck without calling in help. I shouldn't have encouraged you to follow him."

Sean tilted his chin to look straight up as if he could see into the sky. "It's not your fault. I really thought we had him."

"I know," she said softly.

"This whole faith thing can get hard to keep up when I see so many bad things happening around me. I try to stop it and..." He leaned his head against the backrest. "I thought this whole relationship-with-God thing would mean life would go a little more in my favor."

"I know." Ivy sighed. "I pretty much complained the same sentiment to Minnie a couple months back."

He raised his left eyebrow, always the left one when he was surprised. "Did she have any words of wisdom?"

The memory made her laugh. "She said *as long as I've already made my requests known to Him, I try not to complain with the same mouth and lungs He created for me.*" Ivy tapped her knee. "The rest I can't quote verbatim. It was classic Minnie. Maybe I'm not mature enough in my faith, because it's still pretty hard to remember that I'm not alone."

The last word caused her voice to crack. Sean eyed her, as if suspicious of the cause.

"Sean, I should tell—"

"Ivy, there's something—"

The use of each other's names when they'd simultaneously spoken caused them both to stare at each other. "You first?" she asked.

A gunshot suddenly rang out and the impact hit the window. A white circular bit of plastic bulged inside, and the glass fractured around it like a spiderweb. Grace's bark stung her eardrum. She flinched and pressed back into the seat. Then another bullet hit the windshield, and she sent a panicked look Sean's way.

"Don't worry. The windows are bulletproof." He grabbed his radio. "Under fire! Need assistance. Now!"

Helena replied, but Ivy couldn't make out anything she said because of Grace's barking. Two more bullets impacted the shield. Nothing but white on the windshield now, and the plastic-looking layer warped inside.

Her insides shook involuntarily. She kept telling herself Sean was right. It was bullet-proof, but it was hard to stop flinching.

"Grace, quiet!" The dog whined but obeyed Sean's order. He clicked the side of the radio. "ETA?"

"Dispatch says five more minutes, and I'm changing my tire. Hang on," Helena said.

The color in his face drained as he slowly put the radio back in its holder. The glass pinged with three more shots. He reached for Ivy's hand.

She wrapped her fingers around his, and the tension around her gut eased slightly. "How many bullets can this withstand?"

He squeezed her fingers, then quickly released. "Five," he whispered. He moved his hand to the gun on his holster.

"He's already shot more than that!"

"Stay in the vehicle with Grace." His voice sounded strangled.

"But you can't even open the door."

He nodded and pressed the button to roll down the window.

ELEVEN

Sean's heart pounded in his chest. He should've never admitted to knowing how many bullets the window was certified to withstand. "It's the minimum amount. Don't worry." He didn't have time to see if she believed him. He was worrying enough for the both of them. The layers of glass and plastic that molded together to absorb the impact of each bullet made it impossible to see out the windshield. Add the mud splatters to the mix on the side windows, and he felt blind. The shooting had stopped, which meant there was a possibility the ATV driver was approaching. Sean couldn't let that happen.

The driver's-side window rolled down enough for the breeze to hit him fully in the face. He planted his elbow on the window seal and used it as a pivot point to launch up and out of the car, instantly training his weapon to the west, where he'd last seen the

ATV. The sun reflected off the black shield of the helmet, the driver pointing his weapon in his direction. Sean didn't hesitate. He shot three bullets. The driver twisted and dived off the ATV. Had he hit his mark?

Sirens reached his ears, but he couldn't afford to look back and see how far away Helena was. He kept his weapon trained on the driver. He really needed to get out of the vehicle to get a better shot and approach.

"State Troopers," Helena's voice announced through the megaphone-speaker function of the SUV radio. *"Put your weapon down!"*

The driver popped up on one knee with his arm raised. He wasn't surrendering. Sean fired two more shots. At this distance, no wonder he was missing. He could barely make out his form. The driver jumped up and hopped back on his ATV.

A car door slammed. Grace whined and scratched at the back door. The ATV engine revved and took off up and over a hill and vaulted over a creek. Luna took off like a shot, her legs extending and recoiling like a powerful spring. She was practically flying, but Sean knew in his gut that the driver was too far off for her to catch him.

A knock at Ivy's window caused them both

to flinch. He twisted enough, still hanging partly out of the window, to see Helena gesture on the other side of the hood. "I see now why some people call it mudding instead of four-wheeling."

Ivy rolled down her window. Grace whined again. Taking pity on her, Sean lowered the back window. The K-9 immediately jumped out and nuzzled her nose underneath his neck, a sure sign she was worried. He rarely ever had to unholster his gun, as that, in and of itself, was considered a use of force. Discharging his weapon was something Grace had only seen him do at the ranges. Working discoveries typically meant the majority of the danger had passed already. Though, given the last few months with the number of traps and assignments he'd been sent on with the team, he was starting to feel there was no longer any normal.

He shimmied his entire body out the window. The wet mud seeped through his pants as he hopped up to standing. Luna was trotting back their way. Helena helped pull Ivy out of the vehicle without Ivy having to sit in the mud as he had. At least there was that. He'd made a bad call pursuing in that way on the unstable terrain. He'd been so desperate. *Why can't You let me catch him? Don't*

You want Ivy safe? What possible priority could You have that outweighs stopping this man, Lord? He blew out a breath and patted his K-9 partner's head. "Good girl, Grace." Eli had told him that when the job weighed him down, he had to remember to make his requests known but then acknowledge he wasn't God and move on. That was basically what Minnie was trying to tell Ivy, wasn't it? Just with different words. Saying it sure was easier than living it. *Lord, please help someone—even if it's not me—catch this guy.*

His shoes fought against the pull of the mud as he stomped around the back of the SUV. He wasn't sure he was ready to handle what the sight of the windshield looked like up close. If he let himself imagine what would've happened… No, he wouldn't let his mind go there. He focused on the ground and tried to stay on rocks as he moved to slightly higher and much firmer ground. Ivy caught his gaze. "It's amazing how much difference even six feet makes in the tundra."

A hard-earned lesson. "I suppose that's why you have to be a certified pilot to get stationed out here."

The dogs both perked their ears. Helena smiled. "The Nome police agreed to send out their helicopter to help us out."

"Is that our only backup?"

She avoided his eyes. "At the moment." In the far distance, a dozer approached but came to a stop a good hundred feet before Helena's SUV, parked behind them and to the south. "He's waiting to see if it's safe to help out, I think."

Sean glanced out at the hills. "I didn't see a long-range rifle on the suspect, but let's have him approach with caution."

Helena nodded, patted her leg, so Luna would stay by her side, and moved toward the dozer. Grace spun suddenly and her entire back went rigid.

"That's the same scent you caught before, isn't it, girl?" The question being, was it coming from the dozer again or closer?

"Sean, I think we're right in the middle of the mining claim mentioned in that ad," Ivy told him, her eyes wide.

Grace didn't relax, though. "Time to go to work," he said softly, testing to see if she really had something. Grace opened her mouth, catching all the scents in the breeze, twisted and then took off like a shot due west.

"Helena, keep Ivy safe." Sean pressed off the muddy ball of his shoe and sprinted, attempting to keep up with Grace. He hurdled over bushes and thorny patches while she glided across the terrain as if it were a smooth track. She paused at a creek and waited for him to catch up.

The sound of the helicopter's rhythmic patter of rotors in the wind grew stronger. He grabbed his shoulder radio and asked Helena to relay to the Nome PD pilot the direction the ATV went and let them know he was pursuing a cadaver discovery to the west. "Please have them do a sweep around us to make sure we can work safely."

Not even a minute later, the helicopter did just that, circling them from a far radius and then a tighter circle before taking off in a diagonal line to where they suspected the ATV driver had gone. He helped Grace find a shallow point of the creek. Once they crossed, the vegetation grew sparse. Not enough water, perhaps, which was a good sign. His eyes caught wheel tracks, wide enough to indicate heavy machinery. Was it possible the killer had hot-wired the dozer and buried the body over here?

Grace ran to the tracks. The hairs on the back of her neck stuck straight up. The scent was stronger apparently. They ran across the tundra for what seemed like a good mile. Grace stopped right in front of a sage bush and circled it three times, before she plopped down to sitting and panted, her tongue flopping out to the left side. Had she found the body?

Sean took a knee. The dirt didn't look disturbed here, though the tire tracks of the dozer were only a few feet away. He peeked under a gangly sage brush and saw packed dirt, almost as if it'd been planted by hand. The man must have used the dozer to bury his victim here and also taken the time to transplant bushes right over the site. In the wild. Where the disturbed earth wouldn't easily be seen by helicopter or drone.

He hated smart criminals.

"Good girl," Sean said in the happiest voice he could muster. He retrieved her toy and let her run off with it, only a few feet away. "Helena," he said gruffly. "I'm going to need the dozer to follow my coordinates. I think we've found something."

"I hope you're right, because it's about time something good happened. The helicopter found a campground and landed to investigate, but there's no sign of the suspect. It appears he's disappeared again."

Sean remained on his knees near the sage because it finally hit him. While he had likely succeeded in his assigned mission to find the victim, he'd just made it harder to convince the colonel he should stay in Nome.

The landscape she usually enjoyed watching flew past her without her really seeing it. "Do you think Grace has really found the victim?" Ivy finally asked.

Helena sighed, hands at the wheel as she drove over the bridge that crossed Safety Sound. The name seemed ironic now. "We'll find out soon enough."

Ivy turned in her seat to fully face Helena even though the woman kept her gaze on the road. "What's your instinct?"

She glanced at her, eyes soft. "I think so, yes."

Ivy faced forward. That was her instinct, too, which meant that Sean had finished what he needed to do. She needed to stop relying on her ex to be her safety net and prepare for what came next. She'd pick up the husky first and then Dylan. Neither one could fit well in the SUV with Luna taking up the entire back seat. "I need you to stop at the mission and let me retrieve my Jeep."

Helena slowed down and pulled off the highway into the parking lot but hesitated to unlock the doors.

"I need my own wheels again. I doubt Luna

is the type of dog that likes to share a back seat with a husky."

"I knew you'd end up adopting the husky. I saw that look in your eyes when we found her at the dredge lot."

"You don't approve," Ivy said.

"What you decide is none of my business," Helena replied. "If I pulled a face, it's only because I know Sean won't like it, but—"

"He won't be here to have a say in that, will he?"

"He told you, then." Helena sighed. "If they've found the body like I think they have, no. The trooper assigned to this post knows this case is high priority, Ivy. The moment he arrives, he's going straight to the campsite they've found to gather evidence and potential leads. We're going to get him."

Ivy folded her arms across her chest. She'd heard that reassurance used too many times to mean anything. "Is the mission cleared for use now? Would I even be allowed to move back in?" She'd loved her little home, but now the cozy store and apartment brought her a shiver of trepidation, and she hated it.

"As soon as we know you're safe."

Ivy grabbed the Jeep keys she'd kept in her purse. "Okay."

"I'll follow behind you all the way until we get you settled back at the bunker."

Ivy stepped out. The sound of tires on gravel made her spin on a dime. A mud-covered SUV with the windshield missing pulled to a stop. Sean stepped out with Grace trotting behind him.

"Looks like a pretty chilly ride." Her attempt at humor failed.

He shrugged as he strode up to her. "Grace and I both have coats. She seemed to enjoy the wind in her fur. What's happening here? Another break-in?"

"No, she's getting *her* Jeep," Helena said, one foot out of the intact black SUV. "I was going to follow her, but if you want to, we can switch vehicles. I'll take that back to post."

Ivy held up her hands. "That's not necess—"

"That'd be great," Sean said.

Helena looked between the two of them and settled on Sean. "News?"

"Grace has never been wrong." His voice sounded ragged. "The stationed trooper arrived with a couple of Nome PD deputies. They're processing the scene and asking the helicopter pilot to stick around a couple more hours. See if they'll spot anything."

"So we were right, then. This is about gold.

The mining claims…" Ivy's words trailed off as she tried to connect the dots.

"Likely, but we still aren't sure how."

"The mining claims were for sale, right?" Ivy turned to Helena, whose eyes lit up.

"The two men in the B and B."

Sean frowned. "The guys that wanted to buy…" His confusion cleared. "Oh, the men that were looking to invest in some gold mines."

"Exactly." Helena beamed. "I can stop by the B and B after I pick up a new vehicle from post. I'll see if they are still in town and let you know." She led Luna to the shot-up SUV, carefully backed up and moved on down the highway.

"It was definitely her?" She felt silly the moment she asked, but some part of her needed to hear it.

He gave a curt nod. "The rolled-up rug just as you described."

Ivy felt a tug in her gut. She crossed the space between them and wrapped her arms around him. His back stiffened, but his hands slipped around her waist.

"I'm okay, Ivy," he rasped. "It's my job." But she felt his spine and shoulders relax. His arms wrapped tighter around her, and he sighed deeply.

"Maybe it's more for me, then," she whispered. They stayed in the embrace, and she rested her chin on the top of his shoulder. "I don't think I'll ever forget seeing Francine and the realization it was too late to save her. But I knew I couldn't focus on that if I was going to get her justice." She straightened and stepped slightly back. "Is that a little what it's like for you?"

"Almost exactly." His hands dropped from her waist, and it was as if they were on their first date again. Awkward and unsure of what to say or do next. He turned and walked to the Jeep.

"Did you find it odd the way Helena emphasized that it was *my* Jeep?"

Sean shook his head and bent over to peek underneath the vehicle. "No. It was her way of reminding me that we're not married. I can't boss you around."

For some reason, the notion tickled her. "Have you ever really bossed me around? You had strong opinions, of course—"

Sean dropped in a squat and looked up at her, the beginnings of a smile at the edge of his lips. "No. I knew you well enough to know you'd make up your own mind and do what you wanted." He stood and wandered to the other side of the Jeep, taking a look underneath again. "Besides, you had me wrapped around your little finger and you knew it."

The sentiment evaporated all humor. "I think it was obvious I couldn't boss you around, either."

He moved to open the back door, peering inside. "No," he said quietly. "I suppose you're right about that. We both were too stubborn." He lifted his gaze to meet hers. "I thought my job as your husband was to keep you safe, and I'm sorry that didn't extend to more than your physical safety. I know I didn't cherish your heart like I should have." He coughed and moved to check underneath the hood. "The Jeep doesn't appear to have been compromised. I'll follow you."

Ivy got into the Jeep and focused on the musk oxen that were grazing a few hundred feet away. They offered her a sense of normalcy when her stomach twisted into knots. His apology should've brought her peace, but instead her throat tightened, fighting off tears. She turned the ignition on and spun the car onto the highway. A husky and a toddler boy were waiting for her. They were her true home now.

Twenty minutes later, she walked out of the vet's office with the beautiful husky. "What should I name you?" she asked, letting her fingers sink into the dog's soft fur, gently massaging away the tension in the husky's neck. The dog looked up adoringly and twisted to lick her arm.

Sean waited in the parking lot, leaning against the black SUV. "You're sure about this?"

"I don't understand why you're so against it."

He rolled his eyes. "You're hiding out from a killer in a survival bunker with a foster baby. Why not adopt a dog, too?" His sarcasm was evident, but he shook his head as if he'd disappointed himself. "Sorry."

The only thing she was sure about was not letting this beautiful animal go another day without good care and love. And, selfishly, the dog would help her feel safer after Sean left. Grace harrumphed but remained firmly at Sean's side, even as the husky strained against the leash to smell her.

"Ivy?" a man called out. She looked up to see Nathan gesturing to her from across the street. After she waved back, he jogged in her direction.

Nathan's forehead was creased and sweat gathered in the hollow of his neck, presumably from the run he appeared to be taking. "Is it true? Mom said they found her..."

Ivy glanced at Sean for permission. She didn't want to make a mistake in revealing something she shouldn't.

"I'm afraid so," Sean answered, compassion in his eyes. "Can I ask how you heard?"

"My mother knows the helicopter pilot's wife. She knows everyone." Nathan's head fell, sorrow written all over his features. His bright eyes focused on the husky Ivy fought to keep by her side. "Sky?" he asked.

"You know her?"

"It was her dog." His voice cracked. "Sky never warmed up to me, though. Olivia said she wasn't that fond of guys in general."

"You were a little closer to her than we knew." Sean regarded him with a shrewd eye.

Nathan's eyebrows pulled in tight. "Yes, we were close. I didn't want to upset my dad further."

"Did you know she was planning to steal gold from your family's business?"

Nathan gave a side-glance to Sean, then turned back to Ivy. "Olivia said she wasn't going to go through with it. She'd gotten herself entangled in a mess, but she said she was taking care of it. On the day she went missing, she left me a text—" His voice broke and he pressed his free hand against his eyes for a moment.

"What'd the text say?" Ivy asked gently.

"She needed to disappear and lie low, but she'd text me where to meet her. She said she'd make things right and not to worry." Nathan squatted and reached out to pet Sky, who rested her chin on Nathan's knee, the dog's soulful eyes looking up at the man. "She told me to keep my dad calm."

"That's why you were trying to convince your dad that maybe she didn't steal anything."

"I tried to cover for her as long as I could, but my dad…" He sighed. "I tried to get her to tell me what kind of trouble she was in, but she wouldn't tell me. I should've insisted."

"Did she mention any other details? Any names?"

He shook his head and turned his face away. "No. Nothing like that."

"Did you know her before you hired her?" Ivy asked.

He cleared his throat. "No. I think she'd never had a good employer before. Or she didn't want to get too close to us before she stole from us, but I watched her change before my eyes. Her heart changed." He exhaled a long breath. "I have to believe she would've done the right thing in the end."

"You can help us get her justice by giving us your statement," Sean said.

Nathan nodded rapidly. "I should've done that earlier. This will hurt my family, knowing I essentially let someone steal from them. I really did think she was going to bring it back in a day or two."

Sean's stern expression softened. "We may have what she stole. Your testimony should help get it back more quickly."

The other man's eyes widened, but it didn't ease the tormented expression on his face. "I'll stop by the trooper post today." He glanced down at Sky. "I'm glad you're getting a good home." He turned and jogged away, albeit at a slower pace.

Ivy turned to pat Sky on the head. "I'm glad I know your name now. It suits you."

Sean's radio came to life. He picked it up to answer. Helena's voice was coated with static but still clear. "The two men are still here. How fast can you get Ivy to the B and B? I could use her help."

Sean looked to Ivy, the question in his eyes. What possible reason could they need her? But she would never turn down a chance to help end this nightmare, so she nodded. "We'll be right there."

TWELVE

"I've been thinking. That's twice now our suspect has gotten away by ATV." Sean walked with Ivy from their parking spots on the side of the road to the B and B. Sky remained on Ivy's left side as Grace stayed on his left. "As a survivalist expert, how—"

"Is he able to hide? He knows the area well. If you do, it's easy to disappear," she told him. "Given his knowledge of traps, he definitely has survivalist skills. I imagine he only learned the skills to evade law enforcement, but that's going against your rule of making assumptions. I also can't claim to know what he'll do or where he'll hide next. Sorry."

"I should've argued for Gabriel to stay longer."

She quirked a brow. "Isn't he helping with Katie's case?"

"Yes, and I want that solved for her sake,

but if we'd had Bear here, we might have gotten the suspect's scent at the campsite."

Ivy gestured in front of her. "There are hundreds of miles of hiding spots around here. An ATV can cover more ground than Bear could possibly in one day. I'm sure Gabriel would tell you the same thing."

"Arguable."

"Fine, but Gabriel even told me that he and Bear do more rescues than tracking bad guys. Don't beat yourself up." Ivy smiled. "I know you're doing everything you can to help me."

Was she softening toward him? The more time he spent with her, the less he remembered the reasons for their divorce and the more he remembered the good times. His thoughts kept ruminating on Ivy and Dylan. He couldn't stop thinking about both of them. How would he be able to focus on any other case if he was sent back?

They stepped inside the inn's lobby. Helena and Luna rounded the corner. "Oh, good. I'm not sure how much longer they're willing to stay. It's Evan Rodgers and Hudson Campbell. The same two men Fiona pointed out to us at breakfast, Ivy." Helena gave a quick nod of acknowledgment, but her eyes drifted down to the husky. "Is she trained?"

Ivy shrugged. "I assume so? She only

strained when she saw someone she knew. Otherwise, she's stayed by my side."

Helena raised an eyebrow. "I told the men I had a few questions, and they wanted to know if they needed a lawyer."

Sean took a step forward. "I thought they were city types. Either that, or they have reason to be nervous."

"I've assured them they aren't under investigation." Helena's eyes twinkled with mischief. "*Yet.* In any event, they've agreed to wait a few more minutes. I told them I needed to check on something."

"We know from Fiona they're here to buy mining claims," Ivy said. "Have they told you which one? The Bozsan district?"

Sean shook his head. "We can't use any leading questions."

"Besides, they were tight-lipped," Helena added. "Here's why I needed you, Ivy. Because of our time crunch, I'd like you to make the emotional plea. Reveal you're in danger and make them feel like heroes if they help with information."

Ivy pulled her chin back and blinked. "That wasn't what I was expecting. Are you asking me to flirt?"

"No," Sean answered quickly. His neck felt hot. "I'm sure she wasn't."

Helena shrugged, a laugh playing on her features. "I was thinking more about having you describe the suspect for them."

Fiona rounded the corner with a stack of white towels in her arms.

Ivy approached and took the top half off the stack to see Fiona's glowing face. "Let me help you with that." She set the towels on top of the countertop. "Fiona, can you tell us any more about those two men interested in gold claims?"

The innkeeper leaned forward and peeked left and right. "Well, I don't know much about our guests, but my Ben did try to give them some advice. Mostly, they wanted to know where to find reputable employees." Fiona threw her hands up in the air and rolled her eyes. "If that were easy, everyone in Nome would be rich and never get swindled."

Sean studied Fiona's countenance. So the woman knew about the gold stolen from her husband's dredge. Did she know her son had been in love with the thief?

"Between you and me," Fiona continued, her voice hushed, "it seems those two have just come into some money and thought it would be an easy way to multiply their fortune, but Ben gave them the hard truth. They've been holding interviews in my dining room for a crew leader. I've weeded out quite a few that would be no good for them."

"Oh, they asked you to screen the applicants?" Ivy asked.

"No, but I'm sure they appreciated it."

Grace snorted, and while Sean was sure it had to be from the fabric softener smell wafting from the towels, her timing was perfect.

"Anyone come to interview with red hair?" Helena asked.

"Auburn," Ivy corrected. "Over six feet tall."

"No," Fiona said slowly, her curiosity piqued. "The men have also been gathering price quotes for equipment, trailers, that sort of thing. I think they're stepbrothers, but they both must have been in their father's will. Evan wasn't as hot on making their fortune in gold as Hudson, but he's recently broken up with his girlfriend—sounds like she looked a little like you, Ivy—so he was eager to come to Alaska and get his mind off things, you know."

Ivy grinned and shared a smile with Helena. "I suppose that's good to know."

"Sorry I couldn't be more help. Like I said, I don't know much about them." Fiona turned around and went back to stuffing the towels in the back closet. If only every witness *didn't know* as much as Fiona knew.

"Thank you, Fiona," Helena said. "We'll only need the dining room for a few more minutes."

Sean gestured for Grace to stand back up from her seated pose. "How about I take the lead?" He walked ahead, mumbling under his breath. "No flirting necessary."

"What was that?" Helena asked.

He shot her a glare. "Nothing."

The two men in the dining room wore loudly colored sweaters and sat on opposite sides of a table, both on laptops with their phones also in their hands. They looked nothing alike, one with blond curly hair and the other with straight jet-black hair, but their mannerisms hinted at a familial resemblance.

"State Trooper Sean West. I understand you've been speaking to my partner, Helena." He gestured. "And this is Ivy West." He'd let them draw their own conclusions about having the same last name. "Ivy was a recent witness and kidnapping victim. We were hoping a quick dialogue might help us get closer to finding our suspect."

The man on the right, Evan, if he remembered right, jumped up. "We don't know anything about a kidnapping." He ran his hands through his thick hair. "What'd you get us involved with, Hudson?"

"Nothing." Hudson's voice rose, genuine surprise on his face, as well. Which was exactly the mindset Sean wanted when he asked his next questions, all thoughts of lawyers replaced with shock and curiosity.

"To be clear, we have no proof that the Bozsan mining district is related to these alleged crimes..." He paused a moment as the two men looked at each other, recognition and questions in their eyes. Helena had said they'd been tight-lipped as to what mining claims they'd been interested in buying, but this was the confirmation he needed. "We could use your help in arranging a meeting with the district's contact to ask a few questions."

"Are your dogs here to sniff us? See if we helped the kidnappers or something?"

Helena opened her mouth to answer but Sean beat her to it. "The K-9 helped me sniff out a murdered victim in the Bozsan mining district."

Their jaws somehow dropped even farther. Evan blinked rapidly. "I... I...don't know. Maybe we should call a lawyer just to be safe. I wasn't sure about investing in gold, anyway!"

Sean cringed. He'd gone too far and scared them.

"We're only asking you to help us arrange

a meeting with the owner of the claims. If it turns out not to be the guy we want, then you can carry on with business as usual," Helena said, shooting Sean a glare this time.

The two men stared at each other, clearly unsure.

"You'd be helping me," Ivy added softly. "This man keeps threatening me and my..." Her voice cracked, and Sean could see the strain in her face was no act.

"She has a little boy." He pulled out his phone and showed them one of the photos he'd taken the other night. "The suspect tried to trick this little one away from his sitter. So you can see why we're asking the public for help."

Evan gawked at the sweet boy's smile. In that moment, Sean knew they would help. "It was an agent of the trustee. That's what we were told. Somebody inherited the district and didn't have the know-how or experience to run it. We don't, either, but we were going to hire people who did."

"We were supposed to meet him here," Hudson admitted. "Marty Macquoid."

Sean shared a glance with Helena. That name had no leads, which made it highly probable it was an alias. "When?"

"Tomorrow. Ten in the morning. He's bringing proof of the gold found recently. We have someone lined up to see if it's legit. After that, he was going to take us to see the claim sites before we signed the papers and wired the money to the trustee."

"That's very helpful," Helena said. "I'd like to ask that you don't change a thing about your plans. With your permission, we'll have some plainclothes waiting for Mr. Macquoid outside the B and B for tomorrow. We'll talk to him, and if he's not our suspect, he'll come inside for your meeting."

Evan and Hudson nodded dejectedly.

"We'll be in touch," Sean said. "Thanks for your cooperation."

The moment they stepped into the hallway, Ivy's eyes went wide. "You have a photo of Dylan?"

He pulled out his phone. "I meant to send it to you, but then I got busy with cooking. Grace and Dylan were practically posing for the camera." Even now, the sight of the little boy's bright grin was contagious. Grace apparently thought so, too, as she practically smiled whenever the boy was in sight. "We should probably go pick him up now, right?"

Ivy blinked slowly, staring at him as if he'd grown two heads. "I'd like that."

* * *

Ivy kept Dylan on her lap as Sky approached on a leash that Sean held. Grace sat alert but passive. Even if it was their last night together, she wasn't about to refuse his training tips. Helena had offered to make dinner and Luna was snoozing, blocking the entire kitchen entrance.

Dylan squealed with laughter the moment Sky's nose sniffed his bare feet. The dog wagged her tail and sat, eager for someone to pet her. Ivy helped Dylan pat her head. "Gentle," she said, easing the force of the boy's taps.

"We may not know Sky's history, but she seems to like people." Sean patted the husky, as well. "I'd like to see how the other dogs interact with her inside the bunker before I take off the leash."

Ivy nodded. While the bunker was a luxury model, they still had limited space. Three adults, a baby and three dogs felt a little tight.

Sean asked Grace to come. She approached and waited. Sky sniffed her and then tried to place her head on top of Grace's neck. Grace huffed, spun and put a paw on top of the husky's head, slowly pushing her down in a seated position. Ivy snickered. "Did Grace just tell her to lie down?"

Sky was now on the ground, panting, a smile appearing to be on her face. Helena laughed, looking on from behind the kitchen counter. "I think that's exactly what happened. The husky is used to a pack leader. Seems to me she's accepted Grace as that leader without a fight."

"I'm glad for that."

"Dinner's served," Helena said. She put out a pot of soup and a set of bowls on the countertop. Ivy eagerly scooped a ladle's worth in a bowl. Once it cooled, Dylan would be able to enjoy it. As they sat at the round table and ate in silence for a few minutes, Ivy wondered at how the awkwardness of sharing such tight quarters was lessening so quickly. Maybe because she'd known Helena prior to this, but it was almost like having a family dinner.

"So maybe we should discuss tomorrow's plan," Sean said. "Do you mind if I call the team to discuss this?"

"Of course not," Ivy answered. She stared at the swirling carrots and potatoes in her bowl, stirring them faster with her spoon. Every time she allowed herself to feel peace amid the circumstances, the reminder of the incredibly high stakes, and that her time with Sean was coming to an end, came at her like flashing neon lights.

* * *

Helena opened a tablet and called Gabriel, who had already spent the day searching for Katie's estranged uncle, suspected of kidnapping the reindeer. They dialogued about tactical suggestions for tomorrow and steps to take for Nome police cooperation.

By the time they hung up, Ivy had fed Dylan his cooled-off soup and a banana puree for dessert. The faux windows on the walls shifted to a nighttime scene. While it seemed like an extravagant addition, she'd been thankful her dad had paid for such amenities to prevent the stir-crazy feeling she sometimes experienced as a child, particularly during long snowstorms.

Dylan's bright blues eyes watered as he yawned. Luna yawned, as well. Dylan giggled, then scrunched up his face and let out a wail. The cranky bedtime blues. She should've known. Minnie had warned her that his naps had been shorter lately.

"Thanks for dinner, Helena. Sean and I will wash up." She wiped Dylan's face and tried to keep the heat from her cheeks.

Helena stood up. "Then I think that's our cue to head for a quick walk before bed." She left the bunker with Luna.

"I didn't mean to speak for you," Ivy said

softly. She unlatched Dylan and lifted him to her chest, the smell of bananas and carrots still wafting from his soft hair.

Sean shrugged. "I was about to offer." He picked up the bowls and walked to the kitchen. Ivy tried to set Dylan down with his toys, but he cried and kicked.

"He's so tired." She tried to hold him in her arms, but Dylan refused to rest his head against her, straining to sit up and move around. These were the most trying parts of motherhood. The moments where he didn't want to sit, didn't want to lie down, didn't know what he wanted.

"Here. I'm happy to take a turn." Sean slipped his hands underneath hers to take Dylan. "What do you think about that, buddy?" The little boy smiled.

"He adores you." The admission slipped out in a whisper.

Sean stared into her eyes. "I think he just likes my low voice." He dramatically lowered the last two words with a grin. "And I think it shocked him enough when I picked him up that he forgot what he was crying about." Sean beamed, and the little boy grinned back at him.

Helena came back inside and stopped mid-stride, spine taut, as if she'd stepped into a private moment. Ivy realized they were standing so close together, as if sandwiching Dylan in a hug. "Thank you for taking him," Ivy said politely. She moved back, allowing Sean to fully hold him without her. He squirmed in Sean's arms, fussing slightly, but not to the extent he had been.

"Maybe he just needs another rousing performance from the musical stylings of Grace and—"

"Oh, please *don't*," Ivy said.

Helena tilted her head back in a laugh. "I feel the same way. It's so special that once is enough." She winked and passed them. "Good night, everyone." Helena pulled her lips in tight underneath her teeth, as if fighting off another laugh. Then she disappeared into her room and closed the door.

Sean's shoulders dropped as he bent down and placed Dylan in his portable crib with some toys. This time the toddler grabbed his blanket and snuggled it, pressing his chubby fingers against the fabric of the crib. Sky was closest to him and flopped against the mesh, as if to accommodate. Grace took the opposite side of the crib and also lay down against it. Smart dogs. "I thought you were a fan of our musical number," Sean said. His tone held a forced playfulness to it, but when he straightened, she saw the slight hurt in his eyes.

"It's not that I'm not," she said. "Dylan usually loves his nighttime routines, and I don't want to get his hopes up that it's a new one that will happen every night." She turned back to the sink, blinking rapidly. It was going to be hard enough to say goodbye to Sean again.

"Oh." His voice sounded as dejected as hers.

"He normally settles down pretty fast in his own crib, but with all the changes…"

Sean joined her at the sink. "I think he picks up on the stress everyone is feeling, even though we try to hide it."

She picked up the dishrag and rinsed out each bowl. The two of them worked side by side, cleaning and putting away dishes. Everything was okay until the moment they brushed up against each other trying to get to the refrigerator and compost bin. Her throat ached with longing for his arms to wrap around her again, like he used to do in the kitchen after a long workday. She'd listen to the beating of his heart with one ear while the other listened to the tidbits of his day. Only now, she realized just how much he'd kept to himself.

Sean spun around and grabbed her hands. "You're shaking."

Her trembling hands were betraying her. "I…uh…must be more tired than I thought."

"Understandable." Sean took a step closer, his fingers still gently wrapped around hers. He looked over her head. "Dylan and the dogs both seem to be sleeping now." His eyes lowered to her lips.

Her heart snapped to high speed, the pulse vibrating in her throat. His right hand lifted, and he trailed his fingertips along her jaw. She leaned forward and slid her hands around his neck and into his hair. Why did his touch have to feel like she'd finally returned home? His eyes met hers and he lowered his head, his lips brushing against hers ever so softly. She leaned into the kiss, refusing to think of the consequences.

Grace whined. They broke apart, her heart racing. Grace's eyes were still closed, but her paws were moving in unison. Sean chuckled. "She's probably dreaming she's running after a squirrel."

Wherever the dog was running, Ivy knew Grace was alongside Sean, even in her dreams. Reality settled in the pit of her stomach. "I know you're leaving tomorrow."

His face blanched. "You heard?" He shook his head. "You always had good hearing."

"And you never learned to whisper properly." She did her best to offer him a grin. Why'd she let her guard down? Kissing him was the last thing she should've done.

"I don't have to go. I'm definitely not going if we don't catch the guy at the sting." His forehead creased. "Not right away, at least."

And there it was. "We both know you can't abandon your team. And with the missing pregnant woman and killers on the loose, Katie's missing reindeer and Eli's godmother's final request, I think it's fair to say you're very much needed."

"You're right, but…" His sigh hinted at conflicted emotions. Were they the same feelings she battled? "I made some calls when I followed you back here. Did you know you can apply to foster Dylan elsewhere? Given the situation and with a trooper recommendation, I'm hopeful the request might be expedited."

"Where would I go?" She watched him carefully. She did not want to have the same fight about Anchorage.

"What if you went back to working that job you loved?"

Her jaw dropped. "Survival instructor?"

She didn't think he'd suggest that. "I have thought about that in the past, but I need something more conducive to motherhood. I couldn't go on trips."

"Like I said, I made some calls. There's a company that needs a training instructor, on site, days only. And I don't need to live in Anchorage. I didn't understand that when I first took the job with the K-9 Unit. I get sent everywhere. As long as my home base is within an hour or so from the headquarters, that's good enough."

"What are you saying?" Ivy's voice cracked.

"I saw you light up whenever you were out in nature. You'll want to share that love with Dylan. That survivalist company is in Palmer, less than an hour from Anchorage. Super small town surrounded by wilderness, next to Lazy Mountain and the Matanuska River."

She held her breath, refusing to consider what really did sound perfect. Rose-colored glasses, likely. She needed some time away from him. She braced herself, determined to ask the question most on her mind. "And how does where you live factor into this conversation? Dylan and I are a package deal, Sean. He calls me Mama—" She turned away to get a glass of water.

"I'm not asking you to give up being a mom, Ivy." His voice sounded more tender than she'd heard in years.

She couldn't look at him, so she continued to face the sink. "Then what—" She shook her head. "Even if you've come to your senses and realized you'd be a great father, we still had problems. I mean, look at us now, arguing..."

He placed his hands on the back of her shoulders. "We're not yelling at each other. We never have. We've disagreed, sure—"

"They were *fights*, Sean." She turned to face him, a little caught off guard that he didn't step farther back. "Let's call them what they were, and face the fact that happy couples don't..." She let her words fail her, shocked by what had almost slipped out of her mouth.

Sean raised an eyebrow. "Happy couples don't fight? Is that what you were going to say? Ivy, is that what you thought about us? Was that part of our problem?"

"No. I mean, I know it's good for couples to disagree." Ivy averted her eyes. Logically, she knew that, but she didn't want to admit how recently she'd learned, thanks to her foster parenting classes, disagreements were actually healthy. How would their marriage have been different? Not that the answer would do any good now.

"I know I was guilty of not telling the whole story when we did argue." He exhaled. "That wasn't fair."

She braced herself to meet his eyes. "Are you telling the whole story now? What exactly are you implying about moving? What are you asking me?"

His eyes dropped and eyebrows drew together. "I... I'm not sure yet. I just know that I want to keep you safe. I want to keep *both* of you safe."

Despite her best intentions to keep her guard up, his admission was like a knife spearing her heart. The only reason he wanted her to move was for their safety. She'd hoped for things she could never have.

A door creaked open behind them. Helena stepped out, her lips pinched. "I'm sorry if I'm interrupting."

They both faced her. Ivy plastered a fake smile on her face. "No, we were done talking. Can I get you anything?"

Helena shook her head and turned to Sean. "Fiona just called me. The two businessmen just checked out of the inn and left town."

Sean bolted into action. He threw his uniformed shirt back on over the navy T-shirt he'd been wearing during dinner. "I'll see if they're still at the airport."

"We can't force them to help us, Sean," Helena said.

"I'm fully aware, but I at least have to try to convince them." He grabbed his holster and made fast work of wrapping it around his waist.

Grace looked at Dylan before glancing at Sky. Her eyes seemed to say, *Take care of him while I'm gone.* Her white tail curled and her spine was alert. The Akita clearly understood she needed to go to work. She leaped after Sean before he even tapped his side, and they disappeared out the bunker door.

Ivy didn't need further explanation. The sting operation wasn't happening. She wasn't safe in Nome, and her heart wasn't safe with Sean. The only way to survive would be to take Dylan and run away. But even then, would they really ever be out of danger?

THIRTEEN

Sean paced outside the bunker. The morning air and movement helped him think, especially since he was short on sleep after the late night at the Nome airport. The two investors had already grabbed the last commercial flight to head back to Anchorage that only happened twice a day. And from there, they would journey on to Seattle.

He wasn't even afforded the chance to ask who they'd told about the sting before they left. For now, he would stick to the plan and hope there was a chance that their suspect would still show at the B and B. As he stewed on it, he realized the B and B owner might be able to shed light on the investors' fast departure. He texted Helena, who was still packing up in the bunker. She replied with Fiona's number.

"Well," Fiona said after answering, "we pride ourselves on guest privacy, but I will say they seemed awfully spooked before they left here last night."

"Spooked? How so?"

"It was odd. They had dinner, and I applauded them on all the research and hard work they'd done. Told them maybe if all the miners had done their due diligence, then maybe there wouldn't be so many failures. Then I listed all the recent districts that have shut down. Next thing I knew, they were giving each other looks like daggers. Hudson said something about danger and cons and stormed out of the room, mumbling about mutual funds looking better every second. They left thirty minutes after, clearly annoyed with each other."

Sean didn't know whether to laugh or scream. "Did you by chance mention anything about the Bozsan mining district?"

"Oh, yes! That was probably the third one. It's an interesting one because it used to be a huge success, but it's all dried up now. Sad. The owner was a respected man but a loner. No family that I knew of. Died alone after spending his fortune on trying to find more gold, ironically."

"Do you know if Evan and Hudson met or talked with anyone in the last hours they were there?" he asked.

"Just you."

"You've been a great help, Fiona. Thank you."

"I don't know how I could've helped, but you're welcome. After you and the officers are done with your little stakeout, you come in and get some hot cocoa, okay? It's supposed to snow today."

Sean shook his head in disbelief and signed off. At least Minnie had kept her promise and not shared with the family the details surrounding the case. If Fiona knew they were after a murderer, surely she wouldn't refer to it as their *little stakeout*. And yet he already felt fondness for everyone he'd met in the community. No wonder Ivy enjoyed small-town life.

At the thought of losing her, his insides twisted in knots. So why couldn't he ask her to give them another chance? Why did he have to dance around it?

The door opened and Helena and Luna strode out, heading for their SUV. Ivy ran out behind her, Dylan on her hip and Sky on one side. Grace made a pawing action. The husky reacted by sitting at attention, waiting patiently, as if it were perfectly normal to take orders from a K-9.

Ivy thrust a thermos toward him. "I wanted

you to take this with you. It's full of hot cocoa. It's supposed to snow later this morning."

"Would it surprise you to know Fiona offered me hot cocoa, as well?"

She laughed. "First snow of the season demands cocoa."

Dylan beamed at him, then turned and put his palm on Ivy's cheek. Sean's insides melted at seeing the interaction. He wanted nothing more than to pull them both into his arms. Instead, he nodded curtly. "Are you sure you feel safe here?"

"I'll put the security system on the moment I'm back inside. I have Sky with me and weapons." They stared at each other for a second until Ivy's eyes widened and she tipped over, straight into his arms. He caught her easily, pulling them both to his chest. "Something pressed into the back of my knees. I think Grace pushed me over!"

He peered over her shoulder to find Grace avoiding eye contact, standing directly behind her feet. "That move is only for taking down dangerous suspects, Grace." The dog seemed to roll her eyes and sway her hips as she took a long arc of a walk around until finally back next to him.

Ivy straightened but Sean hesitated to fully release his arms from around them. The kiss they'd shared had been burned into his memory. "Are you sure you're okay?"

She nodded, her blue eyes peering into his. Dylan had twisted so he could stare at the two dogs below them. Sean felt the tug to draw her closer once more, and he lowered his face toward hers...

"You better get going," she said softly.

Her words jolted him. He dropped his arms and stepped away. "Sorry about Grace." Affection had never been their problem. Ivy had always been his biggest cheerleader. Until she stopped. But she hadn't just stopped cheering him on, had she? She'd stopped living her days with joy altogether. Was it at the same time as he'd started putting walls around his heart?

"I'm sure it was an accident." Her cheeks flushed a glowing pink that matched her lips. She waved and ran back into the bunker. Sky jumped up and trotted after Ivy without being beckoned. Maybe the husky was the right choice for them. She certainly was a smart dog.

Sean waited until he heard the grinding of metal to be certain the extra door was sealed before turning to his partner. "I don't need any matchmaking skills from you." It was hard enough not to kiss Ivy without his dog throwing them together.

Grace harrumphed, clearly unconvinced, and trotted back to their waiting SUV. Helena offered a thumbs-up from the inside of her SUV and started her engine.

Sean opened the door for Grace. "Let's go get this guy."

Ivy cleaned to the sounds of Sky's paws tapping across the length of the bunker, running after the tennis ball Dylan had thrown from inside his portable crib, followed by the tyke's giggles when Sky dropped the ball back inside the crib. Good thing she had a change of fresh sheets on hand before he took his nap. But the extra work was worth the smiles and bonding time between the dog and Dylan. At least it confirmed her suspicions that Sky loved people. She knew it the moment the poor thing had tried to find help for her owner.

Even Sean had seemed to recognize that it was a good decision. She spun around in a slow circle. Wasn't there something else she could clean? She didn't want to think about her conversation with him last night, the danger he was in today. Her fingers drifted to her lips.

He had almost kissed her. *Again.* And she was ashamed about how disappointed she was that he hadn't. They had unintentionally gotten back to a few of the routines they used to share. Cleaning the kitchen together, for instance. They'd done that whenever he was home for dinner. It was habit to kiss back then. Plain and simple. Didn't mean anything.

Then why wouldn't her racing heart slow down whenever she replayed that kiss in her mind? How many times would she allow her heart to soften? She'd almost thought he was about to ask them for a second chance last night. Only to find he wanted to serve as a part-time security guard for them. For a split second, she'd allowed herself to believe they could truly try again.

Why do I want that but also want to grab Dylan and run away? She closed her eyes ever so briefly in prayer. The tennis ball hit the top of Ivy's shoe and bounced to the back of the bunker, close to the laundry. "Mama!" Dylan laughed so hard that he lost his grip on the edge of the crib and fell back to sitting. He rolled over, still laughing, and crawled back up to standing.

Her heart burst and she picked up the little boy and kissed his head. "I love you."

Dylan's humor disappeared, only to be replaced with an intense frown. "Doggy?"

The dog backed away from the ball at the back and turned tail and ran past them, scratching at the front door. She studied the dog. That was odd. Maybe the laundry room scared her? "Do you really need to go out?"

It hadn't been that long since Sky had been out before Sean left, and Sky had definitely taken the opportunity to get things done. Ivy had promised Sean and Helena that she'd stay indoors while they were gone, with the security system engaged. She glanced at the lit panel that operated the system. It was still lit as secure. She leaned closer to examine it. Yes, both the front door and the emergency hatch in the back showed as locked and engaged.

Still, it was a very weird reaction from the dog. Ivy unlocked the gun case, mainly to calm her own nerves. It would only take her a second now to grab a weapon if needed. She lifted a silent prayer that it wouldn't come to that.

Sky's voice continued to warble in sorrowful, urgent tones. She turned and scratched at the door a second time. "Okay, fine. I need to call Sean like I promised, and if he says okay, you'll have to wear a leash. It'll need to be fast, and I can't go chasing after you if you see a moose you want to meet."

She grabbed the satellite phone to dial Sean, but it started vibrating and released a shrill ring. She almost dropped it in surprise. The number wasn't one she recognized, but it could be someone from the trooper post giving her an update. Dylan was also getting increasingly annoyed that Sky wasn't playing fetch anymore. She placed him back in the crib and apologized to the very nervous husky. "One more minute." She picked up the phone. "Hello?"

"Ivy? Oh, good, I finally reached you!" The voice sounded vaguely familiar, but the satellite phone didn't offer the best reception. Sky practically howled.

"Sorry, it's a bit busy here. Who is this?" Ivy picked up the leash and hooked it to Sky's collar. Maybe that would calm her down for just a second until she was given the all clear to take her out. Any moment now, her kidnapper would be caught.

"Anastasia." The phone cut in and out. "Social worker?"

Ah, that was why the voice was familiar. "Of course. Listen, I don't have the best connection, but I have been meaning to talk to you." Ivy rolled her head from side to side, the knot in the back of her shoulder starting to make a reappearance. "Even if the troopers catch the suspect today, I'm considering taking a job in a different area of Alaska. Just to be safe and start somewhere fresh." She paced as she spoke.

Even though she wasn't taking Sean's suggestion to move to Palmer and apply for that survivalist training position, the idea of getting back to the job she loved in a new area was strongly appealing. Besides, she really wanted Dylan to grow up somewhere closer to people. Ideally, she sought a small-town community located near vast expanses of wilderness but not as remote as the mission apartment. Nome simply didn't have that type of employment for her within the town limits. "Can we talk later about the process of how I would relocate while still fostering Dylan?"

She glanced at Sky, who had at least given her the courtesy of stopping the howl but was scratching with newfound tenacity at the door. Maybe she should put down a towel, just in case. Poor thing. She wanted to let her out, but she didn't want to be foolish with their safety, either.

"Of course. Just some paperwork, but that's not why I need to talk to you. I received a call a while back and I'm starting to second-guess myself. You said your ex-husband was a state trooper, right? And he was the one who was taking up your protection detail."

"Yes."

"He called and said you weren't picking up. Which I can see now is pretty valid since it took me a couple times until you answered."

"The satellite phone doesn't always work flawlessly," she admitted. The tension in her neck increased and now her stomach joined in. Something didn't sit right. Sean had been trying to call? Why would he contact the social worker?

"He said he needed directions to meet up with you. And that he knew you were headed north out of town but lost you."

Ivy's mouth went dry. "You gave him directions to the bunker?"

"Yes. I hope that was okay?"

Ivy's eyes darted to Sky again. She knew something. She was trying to warn her. Could Sky smell the murderer? "No, no, no. It wasn't my ex-husband."

"What? Oh, Ivy, what should I do?"

"I... I have to go." She hung up and her shaking fingers hit the preprogrammed number for Helena instead of Sean by accident. The call didn't go through. She cried out in frustration and Dylan's face crumpled in fear.

"Oh, sweetie. I'm sorry. Mommy is just a little stressed."

She moved to press Sean's number again, but the security panel lights flickered. If she hadn't been standing right next to the door, she would've missed it entirely, especially since the perimeter alarm hadn't gone off. Ivy felt her eyes widen as she leaned forward. The lights of the security system flickered again and then went dark.

Sky spun around, looking past her, and released a deep, guttural bark that echoed against the steel walls. No sign of anyone inside. Could Sky hear him approaching from outside? Ivy dropped the satellite phone and wrenched open the gun case. She would trust her instincts. And this time, there was no option to run away and hide. She needed to stay and protect her son no matter what the cost. She grabbed the loaded weapon and stuffed it in the pocket of her jeans. She stepped forward to gather Dylan. Then she'd try again to call Sean.

"I'd put that gun down if I were you." The man stepped out of the shadows from the laundry room, holding his own gun, aimed directly at Dylan.

FOURTEEN

Sean kept his eyes trained on the two men passing each other in front of the B and B. The plainclothes officers didn't so much as glance at each other or the unmarked vehicles stationed around the place. They'd walk around the back where another Nome PD car awaited before making the same loop around the place, this time on the opposite side of the sidewalk.

His right leg bounced up and down. Enough waiting. The guy was almost ten minutes late at this rate, and yet he clung to hope. This stakeout *had* to work.

"When do we call it?" Helena asked through the radio. She was parked at the opposite side of the block. "And you're practically bouncing the vehicle with all your fidgeting."

He rolled his eyes in her direction. "No

need to train the binoculars on me. Let's give it a little longer."

"Lorenza wants a status update. They're about to start a staff meeting. We can join as audio only while we keep our eyes peeled. The team might have some ideas we haven't thought of."

His first instinct was to argue. In the last couple of years, he'd learned to tame the first instinct that claimed his way was the best way. Besides, if he needed to plead his case to stay in Nome longer, then he should stay on the colonel's good side. "Yeah, okay."

He clicked on the tablet mounted on his dash and turned his camera off. The plain-clothes officers rounded the corner. So nothing in the back, either. What if there was another way to enter the B and B? One he hadn't thought of. He was so focused he didn't fully register Helena's update to the team.

"It would be satisfying to still be there when you catch the guy," Gabriel replied to Helena. "But a few more locals have spotted Terrence Kapowski. I think we're getting close."

"If the guy was hiding underwater, we'd already have him," Brayden Ford said, in jest. His Newfoundland, Ella, specialized in underwater search and rescue.

"Hey," Gabriel objected with a good-natured laugh. "Maybe if you hadn't needed my help getting unstuck out of the mud, I would have him by now."

Sean cracked his first real smile of the day. Brayden had the reputation of getting a little messy, but he always got the job done. His radio squawked. Sean hit the mute button on the team feed and answered.

"Nome Police Dispatch to Trooper West. Patching through an emergency call made about an Ivy West. It's from her social worker?" The dispatcher sounded confused.

"Put it through." He leaned forward, his chest constricting as a click was made over the radio. The sound of sniffing filled the speaker. "This is Trooper Sean West," he said.

"I… I thought you called me earlier." The woman's voice trembled. "I called Ivy. She said you didn't call, though. Then she hung up and there was no answer when I tried calling again to make sure she was okay."

He cranked the ignition and turned the SUV around at high speed. He wasn't sure he fully understood the woman, but one thing seemed certain. Ivy was in danger. "What exactly happened?" He flipped on the lights without sirens.

"I gave you—not you, as it turns out—directions to the bunker."

His foot pressed the pedal to the floor, and he struggled to speak. "Thanks for your call, ma'am. I'll check on her now." He disconnected and swerved around other cars to get to the north exit of town. A quick glance in his rearview mirror revealed Helena's lights flashing.

"What's going on?" she asked through the radio. "You're still muted on the team meeting."

He untapped mute just before initiating a ninety-degree turn at full speed. "Possible hostage situation," he said to the team, straining to keep his breathing even. "Our suspect presumably found enough information on Ivy's phone to convince the social worker to give out her whereabouts. She's not responding on her sat phone."

Helena made up the distance between them, taking each sharp curve with him. Another set of lights blinked behind her. "I've got a Nome PD car remaining at the scene in case our suspect arrives. I've instructed the trooper stationed here to assist as backup."

"I'll put the Crisis Negotiation Team on standby until you've assessed the situation," Lorenza added. "Keep us updated."

"Yes, ma'am. About to lose signal." Before

he even disconnected the call, the feed ended. He bumped over the large rocks and ruts in the gravel road as he drove at top speed toward the unusual sight of White Alice on Anvil Mountain.

He grabbed his satellite phone, narrowly maintaining control with one hand, steering as he dialed the number that he'd left with Ivy. His heart raced. First ring. His stomach clenched. Second ring. His breathing grew hot and shallow. Third ring.

"Hello?" Ivy's voice answered.

His foot slipped off the gas momentarily. He blinked rapidly in confusion. "Are you okay?"

"Sure, sure. Just about to get Dylan some watermelon." The toddler wailed in the background and Ivy breathed heavily. "I should go now. He's hungry. Have a safe trip." Her voice sounded monotone.

He paused. She had no watermelon. That had been the prank she'd tried to pull on Gabriel until he found out they were eighty dollars with transport fees. And Sean wasn't about to go on a trip. Someone was listening. "Thanks. I will," he said gruffly.

"Bye." Her voice caught and the line went dead.

He hit the radio. "He's there. We're likely

dealing with a hostage situation. Proceed with caution and tell Lorenza to get that negotiation team on the line."

Grace released a mournful whine in the back seat. She may not have understood what he had said on the radio, but she knew when he was hurting. "It's going to be okay, girl. We're going to get her back." He exhaled. *"Please,"* he added as a one-word prayer.

The turn to the bunker was in sight. He couldn't do it anymore. He couldn't keep the shield up around his heart. What had all his caution brought him except heart-wrenching agony, anyway? It had made perfect sense when he decided fatherhood wasn't for him. He could still love Ivy and his parents because they'd already existed, but he didn't need to add new vulnerabilities to his life. Especially given his career.

Now it all seemed like rationale to cover up fear. He needed a different kind of shield around his heart. Faith was supposed to be like a shield, but it didn't mean there wouldn't be suffering. He'd have to cling to the faith that God was with him whatever may come. Easier said than done. But he wanted Him there with him not just in the hard times, but also the joyful times. Sean was tired of run-

ning from the good to avoid the bad. He just
hoped he got to Ivy in time to tell her.

Ivy felt like she'd run a marathon, as hard
as she was shivering. She dropped the phone.
"Why? Why'd you have me answer?"

"It was the only way you were getting
Dylan back." The man's smile turned her
stomach.

"I've dropped my gun. I've pretended I'm
fine. Let me pick him up."

He shrugged but didn't step away from the
crib. She would have to approach, get close to
the man in order to get Dylan. Ivy moved her
eyes to her baby and his tearstained cheeks.
She focused on him, *only* him, as she strode
to the crib. Then, taking a deep, bolstering
breath, she bent over and picked him up. The
man grabbed the back of her hair and pulled,
sending shards of pain through her skull. She
screamed and Dylan's own cries echoed hers.
The man laughed and finally let go. Her head
throbbed.

"I thought you might still have a little sensitive spot there." He tilted his head and considered her. "I could've made it hurt worse."

"What if I get you the jar of gold? You can
go on your way."

"You and your trooper ex-husband have

cost me millions and you think a hundred grand will make up for it?" His laugh sounded hollow. "Oh, yeah, I know everything about you. Amazing what you can find out about a person by going through their phone." He grinned. "Just takes a little technical know-how."

Sky pressed herself against the front door. She'd stopped vocalizing but clearly didn't want to be any closer to the vile man than Ivy did.

"I see you've stolen my dog and turned her against me?"

"Was she really your dog?"

He shrugged. "She became mine after her owner tried to double-cross me, didn't she?" His bloodshot eyes stared at her. "But I'm sick of traitors, so she can stay here and starve to death. You're coming with me."

She hugged Dylan closer.

"Make him stop crying."

Ivy continued to take steps back. She repeated her plea. "I'll get you the gold. You can take it and go far away."

"You're going to get me the gold *and* help me get out of here, sweetheart. And we both know the only way I'm getting away now is with a hostage. You helped the troopers, didn't you? Only a local would've figured it out. You scared away my investors. Yeah, that's right. I've been keeping an eye on them."

"It was your inheritance, right?" she volleyed back. "You tried to cover it up with a trustee and agent—"

"All me." He smiled as if proud.

"Maybe there's still gold there. If you'd just worked the land maybe—"

"That inheritance was a slap in the face!" he shouted. "My father never gave my mom any money while he had it. Not when she was dying, either. Didn't so much as meet me. Ever. I'm taking my fair share one way or another." His voice reverberated on the walls. "Those people you ran off had money to spare, and they don't deserve it if they're stupid, anyway." He pointed the gun at her. "Get the gold and head for the door."

He thought she had the gold in the bunker? She hesitated. If she clarified, he might shoot them. She lifted the diaper bag up and over her shoulder and let him assume it was in there until they were out of the bunker, with more options. He narrowed his eyes. He was questioning if she had it.

"Did you know Francine hid the gold in the gear I needed for him?" She nodded at Dylan. "At the mission. Before she met you outside."

His lips thinned. "I knew she must have hidden it in your shop. I'd followed her straight from the dredge. She thought she could bargain with me *after* she betrayed me. Enough talk. Go."

Please, Lord, help me see a way out.

She turned to the door, opened the first one and looked over her shoulder before opening the second. He'd put on a mask. Her stomach threatened to heave. He'd been lying. This man had no intention of letting them live if he had a mask on. She'd been the only one to see his face.

The perimeter alarm rang out.

"What's that?"

She felt her pulse in her throat. Dylan clung to her shirt, unusually silent, clearly terrified. Sky still shook against the door. The beep had to indicate Sean had come. She didn't know how he would have made it back so quickly, but she needed to buy some time. "Maybe it's the security system rebooting. What'd you do to it, anyway?"

His jaw clenched. "Shouldn't have been able to reboot," he mumbled. "Move!"

He'd also mentioned he would leave poor Sky here to starve. But Sean would return. He'd find her and make sure she was adopted by a good home. Her throat tightened from the tension of not being able to cry. He pushed her back and she rushed out of the bunker.

The moment her feet touched earth his arm snaked around her shoulders. A sharp point pressed into her lower back. It had to be the gun. Dylan wailed.

"Do exactly as I say." The man's loud voice directly in her ear made her flinch. His foul breath turned her stomach.

"State Troopers! Put your hands up!" Sean's voice rang out loud and clear.

The man twisted, forcing her to turn with him. Three SUVs barricaded the only way out, and three officers poked their heads slightly above the open driver's doors they hunkered behind. She couldn't see any way for this to end peacefully. She couldn't turn her head far enough to meet Sean's eyes. Someone was going to get hurt. She prayed it wouldn't be Sean or Dylan. *Let it be me.*

Sean kept his hands firmly on the gun, his finger off the trigger, but only a fraction of an inch away. The man kept his head and most of his body behind Ivy and Dylan. He might as well have been pointing a gun at his heart.

Grace whined inside the SUV.

The first and most important step to hostage negotiation was to establish a communication, a rapport of sorts. He was supposed to use empathy and build trust. How was he supposed to do that when the man held a gun to the love of his life? The rest of the steps included things like patience and active listening and staying calm.

"You still want to take the lead in negotiations?" Helena said in his ear.

The one thing he wanted most was their safety. And despite trying so hard, here was proof that ultimately that was out of his control once again. The wise thing would be to give up that control. He felt it in his bones. *Help me be alert and see our chance to save her, Lord.*

He reached up and touched the earpiece. "No. We need someone to stay calm and keep him calm until the crisis team gets here."

Helena offered the negotiation to Phil, the trooper stationed in Nome who had arrived last. Even though this moment seemed like the biggest failure in his life, an odd peace slowed his heart rate.

The armed captor swiveled, waving his gun angrily. Sean stepped a touch closer to the edge of the door. Ivy's gaze reached Sean, and his skin felt electric. Oh, how he loved this woman, and he'd never told her properly.

He felt Grace brush against the back of

his legs. At least, he thought it was her. Sean didn't dare shift his attention away from the gunman, in case he lowered his guard, in case they got a safe shot. It would be extremely unlikely Grace would maneuver herself through the small space between the front and back seats in the unmarked SUV. This one was a normal Ford Explorer, not a police utility meant for transporting prisoners, but Grace never got out unless he asked her to.

His peripheral caught a flash of fur to his right. She'd just proved him wrong.

"Did I just see Grace make a run for it?" Helena asked.

Sean darted his eyes to the right for a split second. Grace stayed low, running far to the east side of the small foothill. She was going up and over the back end of the bunker. What was she doing? The first day he'd brought her home flashed in his mind, and the way Ivy had loved on her. He'd ordered Grace to protect Ivy and Dylan a few times over the last few days. She knew the command wasn't still in play, but she still seemed determined to protect.

Grace only did that without a verbal command for him.

And his family. The realization took his breath away. Grace knew he loved them.

"If we just got him to lower his gun for a split second, I would tell Luna to attack," Helena murmured.

"Crisis team has just left. Ninety minutes away," Phil said in the earpiece. "I've been given the clear to start dialogue." The crackle of the trooper's external radio speaker being activated caused the gunman to swivel slightly in Phil's direction. "This is—"

"Don't even try talking!" The man waved the gun. "Just back your cars up and get out of our way."

A ferocious growl echoed throughout the valley of foothills. Ivy screamed and the gunman flinched. A blur of fur lunged at the back of the assailant's knees. He momentarily stumbled. Grace then jumped off her back legs and latched on to the man's hand that held the gun.

Ivy glanced down and elbowed the guy in the gut with her right arm. She was able to step away with Dylan still in her left arm.

"Ivy! Run!" Sean stepped out from behind the safety of his door. He sprinted like never before. If he could just get in front of them… The gun was still in the man's hands, despite his shouts for Grace to get off.

Halfway there. He pumped his arms as

hard as possible, his focus on Ivy's wide, fearful eyes and Dylan's head, buried in her chest.

"Drop your weapon or another dog will attack," Helena shouted.

Grace continued her low growl, whipping her head left and right until the gun dropped to the gravel. Sean wanted nothing more than to continue running for Ivy, to wrap his arms around her and Dylan, but instead he turned to the suspect. The man could have more than one gun.

Grace was still latched on to the guy's wrist. He'd never trained her to attack, so asking her to release the same way Helena did with Luna wouldn't work. Helena and Luna and Phil ran up behind him. "Grace," Sean yelled. "Come!"

Thankfully, Grace heard him call over the man's hollers, let go and ran his way, her mouth hanging open, as close to a real smile as he'd ever seen. She was proud of herself. "Good dog!"

Helena grabbed the man's arms, and Phil kicked the gun far away. The moment the man's hands were behind his back, Helena began reading him his rights.

Sean whirled around to reach for Ivy, but she was already stooped over, lavishing praise and thanks on Grace. "Thank you, Grace!

Good protect. Thank you." She glanced up, tears in her eyes. "Thank you, too. I have no idea how you found out or got here so fast—"

"Yace," Dylan said, half laughing with shuddering breaths.

Sean turned toward a warbling bark. Sky bounded in their direction from the bunker, a leash trailing behind her. Someone must have let her out. With so much commotion, had he missed his chance to pull Ivy into his arms and tell her how he felt? Would she even consider giving him a second chance? He didn't deserve one, and he knew it.

She looked up at him shyly. He needed to grab the moment before it was lost forever.

"Ivy…" He wasn't sure how to start, but he couldn't go back to normal.

Her eyes widened, and she dived for him with her free arm. He caught her and Dylan easily. But he felt an unnatural tightening around the back of his legs. At once, he spotted the problem. Sky's leash had wrapped around both their legs, but Grace held Sky's leash in her mouth, with that same fox-like smile. Helena's laughter reached their ears. Phil had placed the suspect in the back of his trooper vehicle. The danger had passed. Finally.

"A little help?" Ivy called out.

Helena waved. "I think you and Sean can figure this one out yourselves. See you back at the trooper post."

"Grace," Sean said. "I told you I didn't need extra help."

His K-9 released the leash from her mouth, and it was easy enough to loosen until Ivy stood straight.

"What did you mean by that?" she asked.

"I suspect Grace is trying to help me find a way to say I love you. That I love you both." He kissed the top of Dylan's head. "I love you and…" His throat went dry as he looked Ivy directly in the face. Her eyes misted, and he forged on before he lost his nerve, before she could let him down without hearing him out. "I love you, Ivy. And I know I'm asking a lot, but if you're willing to give me a second chance, I'd like to take some foster classes and adopt Dylan and Sky *with* you. I'd like to do life as a team and—"

She placed a hand on the side of his face, her fingertips alone making his heart race. She searched his eyes and lifted her chin until their lips were only an inch apart. "I love you, too. With my whole heart." He pressed his mouth to hers, soft and sure. She released the sweetest of sighs and straightened, her face radiant. Sean's chest felt like it was going to explode. Dylan patted Sean's head, laughing, yet trying to peer below Ivy's arms.

Her eyes twinkled. "How do we get out of this?"

Sean twisted to look down. Grace was pressed against their right side, and Sky was pressed against their left side. "I think this is what is known as a group hug."

Ivy tilted her head back and laughed. Sean pointed to the car. Grace stood and ran off. With a few well-timed lifts of his feet, Sky's leash was loosened from around their legs, and she ran after Grace. Sean held Ivy's hand and walked back to the car. His heart had never been so full.

EPILOGUE

Two weeks later

Someone was downstairs. Sky's warbled voice alerted her before the security alert beeped. She was all packed and ready, though. Ivy picked up Dylan and eagerly opened the apartment door to find Sean on the stairs.

"I've already loaded everything you've asked for from the bunker. You packed up here?"

"Should only take a load or two. All the furniture stays for my replacement."

Sean nodded and picked up two suitcases. She followed him down the stairs and outside, where a small trailer waited. She peered in to find the pack-and-play crib and toys she usually kept at Minnie's already loaded. "We should have plenty of time to get it to the dock. My friend who transports cars here says this will all be in Anchorage within a week."

She tilted her head into the sky and looked out toward the back, where the musk oxen grazed. "It smells like snow."

Dylan reached for Sean and he eagerly accepted.

"Doggy and Dada." Dylan said each word with a nod on each syllable, as if introducing Sean and the dogs to Ivy for the first time.

Sean kissed the top of his head. "Not quite yet, little man, but soon. Hopefully very soon."

She laughed, her eyes sparking with joy for what felt like the millionth time. Foster transfer papers had been approved, along with Sean's intent-to-adopt papers, as well. He had already started attending classes a week ago. Thankfully, they allowed him to attend a couple of classes virtually while out on location. And since the Alaska K-9 Unit had added Ian McCaffrey and his German shepherd, Aurora, a cadaver dog, Sean had someone to share on-call duty with. Ivy could scarcely believe it was happening.

"I realized something, though," Sean said to Dylan. "I've forgotten one key thing before I move you and your mom."

She racked her brain about what they might've forgotten. They'd tried to talk every night while Sean was back in Anchorage, and she'd made list upon list of what they needed. Sean pulled his harmonica out of his shirt pocket. Grace trotted to his side and Sky plopped beside her. Ivy couldn't help but laugh. "Another round of 'Twinkle, Twinkle' before we go?"

He began playing the worst rendition of "Here Comes the Bride" she'd ever heard. He swayed with Dylan, who was situated to face her in Sean's left arm. Her baby boy patted Sean's forearm as if it were a set of drums. Grace walked around Sean twice and Sky followed her.

On Sean's final note, Grace and Sky both warbled a horrible off-tune finishing howl. Ivy clapped and Sean's face sobered. He bent over and set Dylan down on a small patch of grass nearest the building. "One second, little man. I need to ask your mom a question. Ivy, I know we've talked about this, but I want to ask *properly*." He sank to one knee and lifted his face up to Ivy. "Will you marry me—again?"

Her breath caught. "I will."

He stood and reached for her, his hands on her waist, pulling her close. Her fingers slipped behind his neck. He searched her eyes, as if wanting to see proof that they were in agreement. She grinned and met him halfway. Their lips touched. She pulled him closer, reveling in the kiss as peace flowed from her head to her toes. Even though they were moving to a different town, being with Sean was like returning home. Dylan's hands found their pant legs. They broke apart to find him grinning up at them with the surety of a child who knew his parents loved him and each other. Grace and Sky stood, wagging their tails. Then Sean swooped down and picked Dylan up for a group hug as the fat snowflakes, promising hints of a beautiful arctic winter, floated down from the clouds above.

* * * * *

Look for the next book in the
Alaska K-9 Unit series,
Yukon Justice *by Dana Mentink.*

Alaska K-9 Unit
These state troopers fight for justice with
the help of their brave canine partners.

Alaskan Rescue *by Terri Reed*
Wilderness Defender *by Maggie K. Black*
Undercover Mission *by Sharon Dunn*
Tracking Stolen Secrets *by Laura Scott*
Deadly Cargo *by Jodie Bailey*
Arctic Witness *by Heather Woodhaven*
Yukon Justice *by Dana Mentink*
Blizzard Showdown *by Shirlee McCoy*
Christmas K-9 Protectors
by Lenora Worth and Maggie K. Black

Dear Reader,

Thank you for continuing the journey with the Alaska K-9 Unit. The other authors and I have exchanged hundreds of emails trying to get each other's characters right. I think the teamwork required in writing this series also helps us imagine the camaraderie our characters have with each other, too. I've come to love this K-9 team and catch myself thinking of them and wondering how they're doing.

While I've never been to Nome, Alaska, I've learned so much about this very unique place. Everyone who has agreed to speak to me expressed the wonder of living in Alaska, and I hope I've been able to capture at least a hint of what it's like to live in the Last Frontier.

My daughter's dogs, Peyton and Moon, have kept me company during the writing process, so Grace and Sky share some elements of their personalities. And, as I live with a family of musicians, the pups definitely love to "sing" along. As such, I've requested noise-canceling headphones for Christmas. Ha! Seriously, I hope you've enjoyed Sean and Ivy's journey to second chances.

Blessings,
Heather Woodhaven

YUKON JUSTICE
Alaska K-9 Unit • by Dana Mentink

With her ruthless uncle sabotaging her family's reindeer ranch, K-9 team assistant Katie Kapowski heads home to help—and thrusts herself into the crosshairs. She needs assistance, even if it comes in the form of Alaska State Trooper Brayden Ford and his furry partner. But with their rocky past, can they work together...and survive?

HIDING HIS HOLIDAY WITNESS
Justice Seekers • by Laura Scott

A frantic call from a witness whose safe house is breached sends US marshal Slade Brooks to Robyn Lowry's side. But when he reaches her, she doesn't remember him—or the crime she witnessed. Now going off the grid until they figure out who leaked her location is the only way to keep her alive...

YULETIDE COLD CASE COVER-UP
Cold Case Investigators • by Jessica R. Patch

When her sister's remains are found, cold case agent Poppy Holliday is determined to solve the years-old murder. But someone's willing to kill Poppy and her partner, Rhett Wallace, to keep the truth hidden. And it's up to them to dig up the small town's deadly secrets...without becoming the next victims.

HOLIDAY SUSPECT PURSUIT
by Katy Lee

After a murderer strikes, deputy Jett Butler and his search-and-rescue dog must work with the sole witness—FBI agent Nicole Harrington. But Nicole's the ex-fiancée he left behind after a car accident gave him amnesia years ago. And unlocking his past might be just as dangerous as facing the killer on their heels...

SMOKY MOUNTAIN AMBUSH
Smoky Mountain Defenders • by Karen Kirst

Someone wants Lindsey Snow dead by Christmas—and she doesn't know why. The only person she can trust to help her is the man she betrayed, mounted police officer Silver Williams. But can they figure out who is trying to kill her...before the holidays turn lethal?

TEXAS CHRISTMAS REVENGE
by Connie Queen

Emergency dispatcher Brandi Callahan believes her missing sister's dead—until she answers a 911 call from her. When the cryptic call leads Brandi to a little boy just as bullets fly her way, she turns to her ex, Rhett Kincaid. But can the Texas Ranger shield Brandi and the child through Christmas?